# HUMAN FOR HIRE (2)

## SOLDIER OF FORTUNE

### T.R. HARRIS

COLLATERAL DAMAGE INCLUDED

Copyright 2022
by Tom Harris Creations, LLC

**Edited by
Lionel Dyck
Sherry Dixon**
Grammarly
And of course…
***Nikko, the Grammar Dog***

This is a work of fiction. Names, characters, places, brands, media and incidents are either the product of the author's imagination or are used fictitiously. All rights reserved, without limiting the rights under copyright reserved above, no part of this publication may be reproduced, stored in or introduced into a retrieval system, or transmitted, in any form, or by any means (electronic, mechanically, photocopying, recording, or otherwise) without the prior written permission of both the copyright owner and the above publisher of this book.

# HUMAN FOR HIRE (2)

## SOLDIER OF FORTUNE

# IN A ROUGH AND TUMBLE GALAXY

RULED BY GUN AND MUSCLE

*When you need the very best mercenary, bounty hunter, bodyguard or just straight muscle, you find a ...*

**HUMAN for HIRE**

# 1

The six dark glistening phantoms rose silently out of the black, inky sea and climbed a ladder to the rickety wooden dock; their armor lit only by the stars ablaze in the night sky and from the glow of a single floodlight at the far end of the wharf.

A special chemical on the faceplates cleared the salty water from the lens, providing excellent vision through the visor, enhanced by the wraparound night vision goggles each operative wore. They moved quickly to the end of the dock, cradling suppressed M88-A amphibious ballistic weapons at the ready. Seeing no one nearby, the six hunkered together at the corner of a weathered wooden shack that served as one of the algae storage houses for the nearby Zepher Field, located only two klicks to the south.

Their comms were active.

"Alpha Team, clear," announced a voice from within the enclosed helmet. Out of habit, he whispered, although it wasn't necessary. Only those on the circuit could hear him. "Deliver the package."

Through the eerie green glow of the goggles, a phalanx of black humps emerged from the sea along the shore to the north of the wharf. They appeared as silent sea monsters about forty feet long by twenty wide. On silent tracks, they climbed the sloping sandy beach until half their length lay on the shore, looking like a dozen beached whales who had lost their way. But these whales knew where they were.

The rounded ends of the monsters suddenly cracked open and moved to the side, allowing for a full company of black-shrouded soldiers to exit from each phantom and scamper up to the rocky breakwater a hundred yards away. They melded with the dark rocks, faces streaked with black and green grease. They carried Xan-fi bolt launchers and not the ballistic weapons carried by the armor-encased squad on the dock. Even so, these were special Xan-fis that had been modified to fire dull red bolts instead of the blindingly white standard plasma balls. They would still leave glowing streaks of red in the air but not light up the night like the 4th of July as would standard Xan-fis.

Everything about the mission screamed stealth, and soon five hundred anxious warriors were staged for the raid on the Presidential Compound a little under four miles away on the north side of the town.

An assault from the sea was deemed the easiest since the roads to the Palace were monitored with bodies and electronics. The President was a paranoid creature; tonight would also prove him prophetic.

"Did you hear that?" asked Indo Saphir. Although his head was completely enclosed by the metal helmet, external microphones picked up every whisper in the night and relayed them to his headset.

Inside his own helmet, Adam Cain nodded. "I felt it, too. It's not your imagination."

"Rhythmic and getting closer."

"It's not one of ours since we didn't bring anything like that with us," Adam stated unnecessarily. As a professional, he didn't let his concern show in his voice, although he knew instinctively that something wasn't right. The repeating vibrations were familiar and not something to be found in the sleepy town of Shores End. The President didn't have such weaponry; at least, he wasn't supposed to.

"We would have known if Creel had *Spiders*," said Indo. "They are a little hard to hide, and surely Dracu would have heard about them."

"That's the problem," Adam said. "Dracu's been flaky recently."

"Define *'flaky'*; it is not translating."

Adam grinned in his helmet. "It means unreliable.

He's been unavailable when I've needed him, and when I have talked to him this past week, he was short with me, as if he had better things to do."

Indo snorted. "What is more important than executing a coup against the leader of your world?" asked Adam's Anserian teammate. "Do we abort?"

Adam shook his head. They'd spent five weeks planning the operation and training the strike force. And now the target was nearly in sight and with all the covering approaches drilled into the heads of the liberators until they could do it in their sleep—or in the dark—as they were about to do.

"Not yet," Adam said. "Indo, stay here with Caper and Dalin. You other two, come with me. I want visual confirmation that there are Spiders on site before we abort. We're not getting paid to call off operations just because we feel a vibration."

Adam rushed off in a crouch along the side of the grey, weathered warehouse, followed closely by his two companions. He'd picked the other five Indies from the personnel files of Starfire Security, having worked with each of them at one time during the three years the company had been in operation. He chose them for their combat skills, discipline and training in various militaries across the galaxy. They were an eclectic mix, and if mapped out where they came from, it would form a spiderweb stretching from one end of the Milky Way Galaxy to the next. The fact that they were all here now, on this moonless night in the quiet coastal town of Shores End on the planet Osino, was a miracle in itself. The other miracle was how quickly and smoothly the operation came together, at least until now.

"Scout to Alpha Team," said a gravelly voice in Adam's earpiece.

"Go ahead, Scout."

"What is this concern you have for a sound? Please explain?"

"We detected what could be a robotic fighting tank called a *Spider*. It moves on six pointed legs and makes a distinctive vibration when it walks. Indo and I have experienced Spiders before. It's better to verify before we proceed."

"The timetable is critical," Scout responded. "Shift change in fifty-five."

"I realize that. Moving to the watchtower for verification. ETA, ten minutes, verif in eleven."

"The teams will be ready to move on your command."

As Adam and his team slipped among the shadows along the side streets of Shores End, he was glad for Scout's assistance. Scout—AKA Wilsom Panasin—had once been a high-ranking officer in the President's security corps until he reached the point where he couldn't take any more of the sadistic manner in which Creel ran his planet.

The world of Osino operated on a massive feudal system, with the President/King conscripting every able-bodied individual into the service of the leader. The planet's sole export was a crop of bioengineered algae that grew in gigantic coastal farms in the shallows just offshore of the island nation, the only large land mass on the planet. Slightly larger than Australia, all seven million of Osino's residents lived here. And since there was no indigenous Prime life on the planet, everyone came from someplace else, even if it were generations ago.

At the beginning of the colonization, life on Osino was peaceful and basic. That was until it was discovered that the magic algae—used across the galaxy in everything from medicine to makeup—could flourish here. Then the population exploded, and the carpetbaggers moved in. Soon, the strongest and most ruthless ruled the planet, and the new natives—often going back five or six generations—were called to serve the economy of the island, even if only a few ever benefited from the one and only cash crop.

With over a thousand people a day dying in the Soak Fields, Wilsom had enough. In a very vocal display of insubordination, he left the service of the President and became a renegade and the planet's number one fugitive. Soon afterward, Wilsom was approached by Dracu Hor, one of the three exclusive export agents for the algae, about leading a coup against the evil President Creel. Dracu would front the money if Wilsom built and trained the army. He agreed, but Wilsom also knew he was lacking in the expertise for such a large-scale operation. And that's when he had Dracu contact Starfire Security and enlist the services of *The Human* and his team of mercenaries.

Adam reached the aging landmark in the center of town, an ancient watchtower that was the highest point in Shores End. After breaking the lock on the door, Adam left his two operatives to stand guard at street level while he climbed the two hundred twenty-nine steps to the crow's nest.

The suit he wore was a combination dry suit, SCUBA gear and battle armor made of extremely durable and lightweight metal polymer of alien design. To the other members of his team, it was bulky and heavy, but to Adam, it was like wearing a sweatsuit. He bounded up the stairs, taking three at a time, gaining the top in less than thirty seconds and hardly breaking a sweat. He was used to Earth gravity and not the Juirean Standard of Osino, which was at least a quarter less. Even then, Adam often kept the internal gravity in his starship cranked up another twenty-five percent above normal Earth gravity just so he'd have no problem dealing with moments like this. The practice had paid off numerous times in the past.

Using the night vision goggles, Adam scanned the

town, concentrating on the area in and around the President's compound to the north. A Spider stood forty feet tall and about that much in diameter; they were hard to miss, especially in such a low-tech town as Shores End. Was there something else that could mimic the sound and vibration of a Spider, he wondered, perhaps a cooling unit or pumping station? He didn't know. But it was better to be safe than—

*Damn!* He didn't even get the line out before he spotted the metal beast reflected in the starlight. And to make his mood even worse, there were three of the mechanical beasts, with the other two revving up and following the lead Spider toward the beach, the same beach where Adam's five hundred soldiers awaited his order to proceed.

That order was not to come. Instead: "Abort!" he shouted. "I repeat: Abort! Three—count them, one, two, three—hostile Spiders on the move, heading for Scout's location. Wilsom, do you read? Abort mission, return to pods."

There was a strange hollowness in Adam's earpiece. When no response came from Wilsom, Adam called Indo.

"Receiving," his second-in-command called out. "Dead on Wilsom's line. I will run a diagnostic." Five seconds later, there was panic in Indo's voice. "Jamming signal. It is not affecting *our* suits, but all the other comms are offline. They know we are here."

"No shit, Sherlock—"

"What?"

"Never mind." Adam could see the Spiders picking up speed. Standing as tall as they did, they could travel over most obstacles, but in this case, they didn't even bother. They were sticking their long, pointed legs into houses and buildings—it didn't matter—and barreling ahead as they made a beeline for Wilsom's position.

"Any movement from Wilsom's troops?" Adam asked.

"Not that I can see," Indo reported. "They are still waiting for your orders."

"Send a runner. They only have a couple of minutes before the Spiders get there. They need to get back in the pods."

"Will do. Sending Caper."

Adam wasn't surprised when the whole of the Presidential Compound suddenly came alive. Hundreds of troops, already dressed in combat gear, were flooding from the barracks as flash cannon carriers on half-tracks were charged up and moving to pick up the fighters. Everyone had been waiting for the orders. This was a trap.

Adam then looked back toward the shore and the wharf. If this was a trap, and Creel knew where and when his troops would be landing, then he wouldn't let them simply slip away back into the dark of the sea. He would have other forces ready to stop the retreat.

And that's when Adam saw the sparkling wakes of a dozen or more speedboats come rushing in from both north and south, lining up about two hundred yards offshore and behind the submersible pods. Brilliant flash explosions shot off from the boats, signaling the official start of the battle. The bolts targeted the pods, which, as previously referenced, were like a line of beached whales. Adam now saw them as sitting ducks.

Explosions rocked the sleepy town awake as startled residents were shaken from their slumber by what sounded like meteor strikes along the shore. People screamed and panicked, some the victims of the rampaging Spiders, others simply running away from the terrifying sounds of battle.

Wilsom's troops opened fire on the dark bobbing boats in the bay, but none of their flash weapons had the range to reach them. And if the weapons on the boats could reach the troops, they didn't reveal that fact. Instead, they laid off at a safe distance, making sure none of the soldiers escaped by sea. The fate of the revolutionaries lay in the hands—and deadly gun turrets—of the approaching Spiders.

Adam was down the stairs ten seconds later. The faces of his two mercenary companions were painted with anguish, along with a trace of anger. This was supposed to be a simple operation against a minor foe and not like some of their more elaborate missions.

This one was turning into a major clusterfuck, even if none of the aliens knew what a clusterfuck was.

Adam's tactical mind was working at full speed. He knew his five hundred troops would be a solid opposition force for the soldiers the President was deploying. What changed the dynamic considerably were the Spiders. They were hardened battle bots impervious to standard flash weapons. Only larger bolt cannon could affect them. That ... and ballistics, such as Adam's team carried.

The problem was Adam's mercenaries were on-site in more of an advisory role rather than part of the fighting force. They weren't even expected to fire their weapons during the coup, so they came with minimal ammunition, something that, if he got out of here alive, he would make sure never let happened again. Fully locked and loaded would be his motto going forward. But they never dreamed they'd be going up against Spiders, not here, not on Osino.

Adam and his team sprinted back to the wharf, unabashedly running down the center of the street, along with hundreds of panicking natives. Transport vehicles now clogged the roads with everyone heading south. The Presidential Compound was on the north side of the city, and that's where all the action would take place.

Code name Scout—Wilsom Panasin—was with Adam's team, having been brought back by Caper.

"All my communications are down," he barked at Adam as if the Human was personally responsible for the debacle taking place. "I am preparing to disperse my troops. If we scatter, we can survive."

"Hold off on that," Adam said. "My team will station ourselves to the flanks of the Spiders and see if we can take them out. They're running ahead of the troops from the Compound. Your numbers are pretty much on par. If we can cancel out the Spiders, you still have a chance."

"We were not expecting such a strong and organized response."

"I know. But if you scatter now, Creel will just come after all of you a few at a time. You won't get a chance like this again, at least not for years. It's your call, Wilsom; they're your troops. I can only give you advice."

Wilsom looked at the anxious faces of Adam's mercenaries, their faces lit by soft red glows within the helmets from the heads-up-displays.

"Do what you can. I will monitor your progress. If you cannot defeat the beasts, then we will head south, into the Southern Grove. The elevation is higher there; we could control the high ground."

Adam nodded. "That's good. We'll see what we can do against the Spiders. The troops from the Compound will have trouble getting your people away from the breakwater. You have good coverage there."

"If you stop the Spiders."

Adam firmed his jaw. "Yes, if we can stop the Spiders."

Wilsom ran off to rejoin his troops as Adam huddled with his team.

"We have two possibilities," he began. "We can try to take out all three Spiders with the limited ammo we have, but that would be a longshot. Or we can get our hands on one of those half-tracks with the flash cannon. Indo, you and the rest of the team, set up positions to fire on the Spiders as they come through. I'll go after a half-track."

"By yourself?" Indo asked.

Adam grinned. "Time to use some of my innate Human abilities. What can I say? You guys have been slowing me down."

Although everyone smiled and set off on their missions, Adam's mercs knew that what he said was true. He was *The Human,* and that was all that needed to be said.

## 2

Adam stripped off the small rebreather unit on the back of his suit; he wouldn't need the diving gear for the rest of the campaign. This made him more compact and even faster in the light gravity. He ran off, not holding back this time. He felt like a gazelle, sprinting through the savannah. Unfortunately, in this case, it was like a gazelle with a cheetah on its ass.

Although the President maintained his residence here, the city of Shore's End wasn't very large, with a population of only twenty-five thousand. Although the battle had only just begun, it seemed as though most of the people were already gone or were cowering in their homes or cellars in fear. No one was taking up arms for either side. They were content to let things play out as long as they were out of harm's way.

Adam could hear the half-tracks—there were four of them—rumbling down nearby streets. Each carried a troop complement of twenty, with the rest of the force coming on foot.

Just then, Adam saw a lumbering shadow pass over him and managed to dive to his right just as a shiny metal spike crashed through the side of a wooden building only feet away. The spindly leg continued into the sky, reflecting the lights from the numerous buildings that had come on since the beginning of the battle. Adam could clearly see the underside of the Spider as it passed over him.

He had his M88-A, and with just the right targeting, there was a chance he could take out the beast on his own or at least immobilize it. The turrets would still be active but limited in their effectiveness. But he could hear the crashing of the other two behind this one. He would let his team take on the Spiders while he went after the added firepower from a flash cannon half-track.

The Spider ignored him, its sights set on the shoreline just north of the wharf. The battle tank could cover the four-mile distance from the Compound to the shore in about fifteen minutes. Spiders were powerful but not especially fast. The half-tracks weren't much faster, but they were deliberately taking their time, preferring to let the Spiders soften the target before they got there. This went for the ground troops as well.

Adam and his people had spent weeks studying the enemy. He knew that the president's troops weren't that well trained or motivated. Esson Creel was elected president six years ago with a popular mandate. Things only went sour when he upped the production quotas on the algae, requiring near round-the-clock work in the Soak Fields. This added demand came from the off-world brokers, as well as pressure exerted by the transport agents, such as Dracu Hor. Creel obliged, even though it caused considerable grumbling and unrest among the population. Even then, there were only the occasional mini-riots and work-slow downs, but no outright battles took place. The bottom line: Creel's troops were untested, with the same being said about Wilsom's force. All in all, it made for a very amateurish coup. And with the enemy—the President—located in one place and with one small military force, it shouldn't have been that big of a deal. After all, Tidus only charged Dracu three hundred fifty thousand energy credits. That was a bargain basement rate for organizing a planetary coup.

But now, Adam and his team were about to earn every penny of it. And then some.

As expected, the small phalanx of half-tracks was leisurely cruising the streets of Shore's End, not expecting any resistance until they reached the beach and the dug-in force behind the breakwater. The four vehicles were also traveling on separate roads, meaning none were covering the others. It made it almost too simple for Adam.

The problem was the twenty troops riding in the back bed. They had battle armor, which was fine against Xan-fis. Unfortunately, for the soldiers, they provided no protection against ballistics.

Adam's M88 carried a 45-round magazine of 5.56 X 45mm cartridges, and he had another two magazines in pouches on his utility belt. At full automatic, he could light off twelve rounds a second, which was overkill in this case. He didn't have a lot of ammo, so it was more judicious to keep the weapon on semi-auto.

He waited until the black-painted vehicle slid past before stepping out into the street behind it and opening up on the troops riding in the back. The sound of the machine gun was distinctive and echoed off the surrounding buildings, merging with the screams of agony coming from the soldiers as the powerful slugs tore into them. This was warfare very few aliens were used to. Most used the ubiquitous flash weapons with their plasma energy bolts. They went poof while Adam's weapon went bang.

He was running at the back of the half-track before the driver could react to what was happening behind him. Then using his Human-enhanced muscles, Adam leaped to the back, standing with his legs wide apart for balance as he finished off the last of the twenty troops.

There were three other operators for the vehicle: the driver, the lookout and the cannon gunner. The driver had gunned the vehicle by now, ramping it up to the head-spinning top speed of around twenty-five miles per hour. The lookout had his Xan-fi pointed out the back window and had already let loose with a couple of shots that went wide. Adam calmly cradled the M88 in his arms and let loose with a quick burst that sprayed the cockpit, killing both the driver and the lookout and blowing out the front window.

The vehicle lurched to the left and crashed into the side of a building. Most of the structures in Shore's End were made of wood, so there wasn't a lot of damage to the half-track, although the entire front façade of the building crashed down on the front of the vehicle.

The gunner had spun the turret around and was trying to aim it down into the back of the half-track, but it hadn't been designed to do that. Out of frustration, he set off a cannon bolt just the same.

Adam had to duck and fall among the bleeding pile of bodies to avoid the heatwave from the bolt. Flash cannon were mainly used in starships. They had about twenty times the power of a standard Xan-fi rifle and with significantly longer range to reach starships much further away. They also gave off an incredible amount of heat.

Seeing that he couldn't take out the deadly intruder and knowing that twenty-two of his companions had been killed by this single soldier, the gunner chose to bail out of the turret. He was about fifteen feet up and jumped at an awkward angle. Adam didn't check, but there was a good chance the fall might have killed him, saving Adam the trouble.

Adam climbed into the driver's compartment and shoved the bloody carcass through the shattered opening that had once been the front window. Grabbing the joystick control, he pulled back, with the heavy back tracks easily withdrawing the vehicle from the front of the building.

"This is Adam," he announced in his helmet. "I have us a flash-cannon platform, but I'm going to need a gunner."

"Indo here. We have engaged the first Spider. We caught it off guard. Two legs down, and the thing is staggering about. We are about half a mile from the breakwater. I'll send Caper to you. He is the fastest runner, well, except for you."

"Good. I'm on—oh, hell—I don't know how to pronounce the street. It's the one with the blue shopping mart."

"He knows where it is. He's on his way. Where are the ground troops and the other half-tracks?"

"The other cannon-carriers are still on their way to you, along with the Spiders. The ground troops are another ten minutes behind. Get me a gunner, and we'll come up behind the Spiders and take out the bastards with cannon bolts up their asses."

"I admire Human phrasing. Crude, but effective. We'll keep this one occupied until you get here."

Just then, another half-track appeared from a side street and ahead of Adam's vehicle. Either having heard the battle or been called by the driver before he died, the other tank was coming to help.

Adam had a problem. He couldn't both drive the half-track and fire the cannon at the same time. And stopping in the middle of the street to mount the cannon turret would leave him a sitting duck. The opposing vehicle had no such limitations. The gunner was already lining up on Adam.

Steering sharply to the left, Adam once again crashed into the front of a building. He felt the heat and the concussion from the cannon bolt that barely missed to the rear. Without a protective windshield, debris from the building rained down on him. And it wasn't just debris; it was a set of floors. The building was old and built of weathered wood and didn't have the strength to withstand having the bottom floor ripped out from under it.

Adam had to steer right to get closer to the side of the building as the entire structure collapsed. The heavy treads continued to propel the vehicle until it exited back onto the original street and parallel to the second half-track.

Adam gunned the motor, crashing the front of the half-track into the side of the other. This stopped both vehicles, which wasn't a help, at least not for Adam since it freed up the twenty angry and armed soldiers in the back to begin jumping onto *his* vehicle with weapons at the ready.

Adam kicked open the driver's door and dived headfirst out the opening. Xan-fi rifle bolts filled the compartment right behind him as Adam sought shelter under the front of the half-track. It rode up high on two thick tires, giving him room to scoot all the way to the other side. He came out on his back, with the M88 aimed up. He let loose with a barrage of loud gunfire that tore into eight of the native troops while others fell for cover. Adam pushed farther out and was on his feet a second later, sprinting around to the back of the second half-track. He dodged a bolt before lifting his weapon and aiming it above his head and into the back of the APC.

There were still troops on his half-track, taking up positions and lighting off flash bolts in a panic.

And that's when Adam heard the sound of another M88 lighting off. Caper was here, catching the enemy from the other side. The battle only lasted another thirty seconds before everything went quiet.

"You have made quite the mess, Captain," Caper said as he rounded the back of Adam's original half-track. "I suppose we have our choice. I choose the one that is not dented and covered in building debris."

"Good choice. Now, let's hurry. How's Indo doing with the first Spider?"

"The tank is down but still firing. It leveled a part of the town within its target scope. We are all staying out of its way; it is no longer a threat. But the others are now engaging."

"Do you mind if I take the turret?" Adam asked. He was itching to get behind a land-based flash cannon. They were magnificent weapons to fire.

"You are in command. As you wish."

---

A moment later, the APC was chugging down the street with Adam sucking the cool night air from atop the cannon turret. He gripped the dual handles and worked the long barrel of the weapon, getting a feel for the movements. He crouched down, pointing the barrel almost straight up. He would have to do this with the Spiders to get a clean shot at their soft underbelly.

The sounds of battle were all around them now. The other two half-tracks had reached the beach, and the troops were engaging the rebel forces along the rocky breakwater. It wasn't much of a contest, with forty of the President's soldiers against five hundred of Wilson's troops. But Creel's ground troops had taken up positions near the wounded Spider, which, although immobile, was still able to fire its flash cannon. The second Spider was on site and saturating the beach with brilliant rounds of plasma energy.

Adam took aim, coming up unseen behind the towering mechanical monster. He lit off the first bolt.

The Spider was thrown up by the impact, causing it to stumble forward as gyros fought to maintain balance. The ass end was dented and smoking, but the six-legged tank managed to stay upright. The turret began to swivel in Adam's direction.

"Shoot it again!" Caper cried out.

"It's charging. Give me a second."

"We may not have a second."

The light on the weapon turned amber, signifying a full charge. Adam was already lined up, but just as he pulled the trigger, Caper spun the half-track violently to the right to dodge an incoming bolt from the Spider. Adam's shot went wide by about a hundred feet, embarrassingly off-target.

"Hold it steady!" Adam commanded.

"And get us killed? I will do my best."

The Spider's weapon could recharge faster, and another bolt lit off from the barrel. This time, Caper was a little slower, and the back half of the APC was blown off. Adam was flung into the air but managed to hold onto the twin aiming rails.

"We have no drive left!" Caper called out. "Maybe time for one more shot."

"I'm going for the legs."

Adam's second shot was more horizontal and contacted three of the beast's spindly legs. Two snapped, while the third bent at an awkward angle. The Spider planted the wounded limb into the ground and began to pivot on that point, remaining upright and with a downward angle on all the combatants.

"Time to go!" Adam yelled out. Now, it was his turn to bail from the turret.

He landed more gracefully than had the native earlier but not far enough away from the half-track to be clear of the bolt that blew the vehicle into scrap metal. Flame and twirling debris rained over Adam as he lay on the concrete street, trying desperately to protect his head with his arms. The sleeves of his shirt were blown off as something large and hard crashed into his helmet, ripping half of it away and nearly taking his head with it. He was stunned, his eyesight blinded by a veil of red.

"Captain, are you all right?" Caper's voice sounded above the din of the battle. Hands were on him, and he was being dragged across the rough road and up to a sidewalk. He was shoved into an alcove of a building before Caper used his sleeve to wipe the blood from Adam's eyes.

"I ... I think I'm okay," Adam mumbled. He ran a hand over his face. There was blood, but his ears, nose, mouth and eyes were all still there, even if half of his helmet was missing. "Help me up."

Once standing, Adam let the dizziness fade. He could see now, and the ringing in his ears was growing dimmer.

"My comms are down," he said to Caper. "Get an update from Indo."

Caper had his visor open so Adam could hear one side of the conversation. It didn't sound good.

"The third Spider came along the shore from the north and attacked our troops on the beach," Caper reported. "Wilsom has the survivors heading south into the forest. Binnoc is down, and Span and Dalin are working to take down the second Spider. Indo is cut off. He's heading for the forest."

Adam nodded. "Sounds like a good idea. With one intact Spider still on the loose, I'd say we can't hold the ground. Get Indo and the rest of them moving. We're leaving."

Caper helped Adam get his balance and headed in the right direction. Adam scanned the broken road and the charred remains of the half-track for his weapon. It was nowhere to be found. But Caper still had his.

The pair ran down side streets, going against the

grain of the city planners, which had all the main avenues heading for the shore. The going was a little slower as traffic jams had resulted in dozens of crashes and graveyards of abandoned vehicles from the panicked natives. But it wasn't long before they were out of the last row of buildings and sprinting up a fairly steep slope to the forest of alien pine and spruce to the south of Shore's End.

Adam and Caper weren't alone. Dozens of others, most dressed in black uniforms and with grease on their faces, were running with them, the remnants of Wilsom's army. As Adam looked around, he was shocked to see only fifty or so out of five hundred. Even as they ran, more were dying. The third Spider, undamaged and fully mobile, was only a few hundred feet behind and firing off cannon bolts every few seconds. Trees were splitting to their core and igniting from the intense heat from the bolts.

And that's when Adam realized what the Spider was doing. It wasn't only targeting the fighters; it was also setting a large swath of the forest ablaze, leaving nowhere else to go but to the south. Adam knew what that meant.

## 3

In a fit of rage, Adam ripped off his helmet. It was useless anyway, having had half of it blown away earlier. He looked around through the blood-tinted sheen at the smoke, fire and devastation wrought by the savage mechanical beast. The forest was ablaze, ignited by myriad star-hot plasma bolts striking all around, and with the whipping flames herding the survivors toward the sea cliffs a mile away.

Almost the entire assault force of five hundred native liberators had been annihilated. Of Adam's six-person command team, he'd already lost Binnoc Owes. Tidus wouldn't like that; he was his employee, and Adam's team wasn't supposed to do the fighting. They were paid to plan and train, not to fight. Fighting would have cost more.

But to add insult to injury, the native military

leader of the now-failed revolution, Wilsom Panasin, only had a handful of his troops still with him and barreling headlong through the forest, along with Adam's surviving mercenaries.

It was not a good day all around.

Indo Saphir slipped up beside him.

"The second Spider is down, but we also lost Span. The last one is still coming."

"I can hear it," Adam confirmed. "Since when did they start putting horrifying soundtracks in the bastards?"

"It is working to scare our troops even more."

"I know. I'll have to keep that in mind the next time *we* use Spiders."

"If there is a next time."

Adam shrugged. There was that consideration.

"We must stop this run," Indo continued. "They intend to chase us over the cliffs."

Adam nodded as he ran. He was much faster than anyone else in the forest, but he moderated his pace so the others could keep up. He also knew his shuttle was on standby, the seventh member of his team at the controls and awaiting the order to exfil. Seeing a small speeder sweep in and extract the mercenaries wouldn't do much for the morale of the remaining liberators. But what the hell? Their time was short anyway. Nevertheless, Adam was confident he and his people could escape. Not all revolutions were destined to succeed; in fact, very few did.

Even so, Adam was frustrated at the utter failure of his meticulously planned operation. But what was one to expect when you were betrayed? He wasn't a hundred percent sure who it was, but he had a pretty good idea: Dracu Hor, the moneyman/being of the operation, the instigator who had devised the coup originally and then financed it out of his own pocket. Why he would do such a thing was still a mystery. Maybe once Adam had his hands wrapped around the alien's bulbous neck, Dracu would provide some answers. When that might be, Adam wasn't sure. All he knew was that no one doubled-crossed *The Human* and lived to talk about it. At least not for long.

Through the smoke and flames to his rear, Adam saw the forty-foot-tall, six-legged tank/gun turret smash through another grove of trees, spinning the flash cannon barrel to and fro, targeting the fleeing troops.

With Adam's team now out of ammo, there was no way to take out the last of the deadly tanks. The outcome of the battle was a given.

"It is almost time to call it," Indo puffed next to Adam. He had ten years of experience being an Indie soldier of fortune, and Indo could see the writing on the wall.

That was the thing about mercenaries. They came

into the game for the money, but if the situation became untenable, they would bounce and live to fight another day … and for another fee. They had no skin in the game.

Not so the poor natives who risked everything at the chance for a better future. Once again, Adam mentally shrugged. Maybe next time.

"All right, make the call," Adam said to Indo.

Relief flooded over Indo's equally bloody and soot-covered face. Originally, his skin was tinged green. Now, it was the uniform black and red of all the other survivors.

"Confirmed," Indo said. The visor on his still-intact helmet was open, allowing Adam and him to talk. Adam's comms were in his now discarded helmet.

"He will be waiting just below the ledge. We may have to jump," Indo shouted at Adam through the roar of the fire, the pop of energy bolts and the ungodly alien racket that passed for music blaring from speakers in the Spider.

"Understood.

Just then, Wilsom Panasin sprinted up next to Adam and Indo.

"It had to be Dracu!" he shouted. "He is the only one who knew of our plans."

Wilsom had once been a high-ranking member of President Creel's security guard until it became too much for him to continue. Now, he was consumed with hatred, not only for President Creel but also for the turncoat merchant who had set him on the path to a humiliating defeat.

It wasn't supposed to be like this. Wilsom and Dracu were supposed to rule Osino jointly after Creel was deposed. And the changeover was to come with cheers and fireworks from the native population. Creel was a carpetbagger who only immigrated to the planet twenty-two years ago. That was when the big push to grow the genetically engineered algae was picking up steam. The algae was Osino's only cash crop, and certain powers ensured the green miracle plant kept growing, even at the cost of tens of thousands of lives per year. But that was all to end once the revolution took place.

As with most feudal systems, once the castle was taken, all the surrounding territory would become the subject of the new master. And that new master was to be Wilsom, with Dracu Hor as his trusted second. Apparently, Dracu had a change of heart.

"We're getting off the planet," Adam screamed at Wilsom. "Are you coming with us or not?"

Wilsom stumbled as he ran. Once regaining his traction, angry eyes bore into Adam. "You are abandoning us?"

"It's not our war. We only planned the assault and trained the troops. We weren't counting on a turncoat to screw up everything."

"Define *screw up*; it is not translating."

"Just what you think it means. We were betrayed. It's time to get the hell out of here. You can live and plan another coup, or you could stay here and die."

"That is no choice."

"You're wrong; it's the *only* choice. But hurry, I see the edge of the cliff in front of us."

"My troops?"

"We only have room for you. Make up your mind."

Adam's four-person team skidded to a stop only feet from the bluff's edge, overlooking a rocky and wave-beaten shoreline two hundred feet below. Hovering about fifty feet below the top was the team's small transport speeder, the shuttle they used between their main ship in orbit and the surface. It was riding on fiery plumes of lifting jets with the top hatch open. Through the front viewport, Adam saw Esnon Yonick motioning with his hands for the team to jump.

"I am unsure," said Indo, looking at the gap, the drop and the dizzying distance to the rocks below.

"You can make it," Adam said. "I'll go first and then help the others."

Even so, Adam motioned for Esnon to move a little closer. He did his best, careful not to clip a stubby wing on the rock outcropping.

Ignoring the indecisive Wilsom, Adam took a casual leap through the air and landed smoothly on the wide metal hull near the hatchway. The jump was a piece of cake for a Human, helped by Adam's superior strength and balance. That was why he went first; the others would need his help.

Next came Carpin and Dalin. With each, they landed hard and then slipped, sliding toward the side of the shuttle before Adam grabbed them and pulled them to safety.

Indo turned to Wilsom. "Your last chance."

The native still hesitated, especially now, looking at the jump he would have to make.

Indo shook his head with impatience ... and jumped.

With his remaining team safely in the shuttle, Adam looked up one last time at Wilsom.

"The fight isn't over as long as one of you lives," Adam yelled up at the alien.

Adam could see the agony on Wilsom's face. But then it changed to pure terror ... and a moment later, he jumped, his arms flailing in the air and a shrill scream coming from his throat.

Adam caught the native without a problem, even though Wilsom clung to the Human, his knees almost too weak to walk. Indo and Caper helped him through the hatch.

Adam stood on the hull for a few moments longer, bucking the constant updraft from the sea below and watching the first remnants of Wilsom's army cast themselves over the side of the cliff in their last defiant act. It was sad and sickening. But there was nothing Adam could do. His job here was done, and not every mission succeeded, even if this was one of the worst losses Adam had ever suffered as an Indie mercenary.

He climbed through the opening and dogged the hatch. As soon as Esnon got the green light on his board, the ship was off and headed out of the atmosphere.

---

The shuttle was closing on the mid-range starliner Adam had checked out two months ago from Starfire Security inventory to transport him and his crew to Osino. Adam wasn't about to use his own ship to house the team. They were aliens, and they smelled. But now, all of that seemed inconsequential. The mood was somber in the smaller craft, with no one speaking. A loss was a loss, whether one agonized over it in a locker room after a football game or above a planet twenty thousand light years from Earth.

"Adam, a link is coming in for you," Esnon reported. "It is from Dracu."

"Dracu … you traitor!" Wilsom cried as he surged toward the pilothouse.

"Back off!" Adam ordered. "I'll handle this."

The bloated, yellow face of the alien/native of Osino smiled at Adam.

"I am glad you survived; I never had any doubt that *The Human* would make it out of that conflagration alive."

"So, it *was* you," Adam said acidly. "Why? You could have had it all."

"But I will, Mr. Cain. It seems President Creel heard rumors of a pending coup and approached me with an offer. You are looking at the new Vice-President of Osino, and with Creel promising to step down in a few years to enjoy his ill-gotten gains on a planet more to his liking. He would prefer to spend his later years on a world with his own kind. I am sure it is a sexual thing. As you know, he was not born on Osino, not like Wilsom and me. So you see, I am destined to become President, just after a short delay."

"Then why the massacre tonight? You could have called it off."

Dracu grimaced. "Yes, that was discussed. However, after some debate, we decided that the revolutionary elements of the population had to be purged in order to provide for more lasting peace. Bringing them all together at one location to be executed seemed the logical choice. It would save time and effort in tracking down each individual rebel. Hence, we decided to let the coup proceed."

"And the Spiders?" Adam asked.

Dracu beamed. "I brought them in on my ships. They were quite expensive and difficult to hide. Even so, I am quite proud of my insight. They helped in the effort, did they not?"

"I will kill you, Dracu!" Wilsom yelled from the passenger bay.

Dracu's eyes lit up. "I see our friend Wilsom survived as well. That is too bad. Did you know Creel was grooming him to be his replacement? If only he had waited...."

"You're the one who approached Wilsom about staging this little revolution of yours," Adam pointed out. "It wasn't his idea."

"Ah, but he began the movement when he publicly left the President's service. All I did was take advantage of the growing discord. Now, I must ask you, Mr. Cain, what are your intentions going forward, you're intentions toward *me*? You must know nothing I did was aimed at you personally. I respect your skill and abilities, as does everyone in the galaxy. Hopefully, you will see this as just another job. Your company has been fully paid, and you survive. There should be no repercussions, should there not?"

"That is how it normally goes. We provide a service, but we cannot guarantee the results."

"Then there is no animosity between us?"

"I didn't say that," Adam snapped, his eyes steady as they bored into the alien on the screen. "All I'm saying is that I'm a professional, and these things happen now and then. It would be unprofessional to hold a grudge."

"Very good then!" Dracu exclaimed. "I am relieved to hear that. It was only business, not personal."

"That's right, only business. Even so, I'm going to cut this link now because I can't stand another second of looking at your ugly, traitorous face."

Dracu opened his mouth to speak ... but Adam cut the line before he could get the last word out.

Adam may have appeared calm on the outside, but on the inside, he was seething. Yes, it was unprofessional to hold grudges. But as previously mentioned, no one double-crossed *The Human* and lived to tell about it, at least not for long. Adam didn't know when or where, but eventually, he would even the score with the traitorous Dracu Hor.

Wilsom was at Adam's side.

"I wish to enlist your services," he said abruptly, his voice deep and serious.

Adam snorted. "Yeah, right. You have no credits; in fact, you have nothing. You can't even go back to Osino."

"I realize that, but I want you to kill both President Creel and that fat worm Dracu Hor."

"Didn't we just try that?"

"I don't mean a coup—a revolution—as before. I mean an *assassination*."

Adam laughed. It had been years since he'd made

his living as an alien assassin, but he didn't tell Wilsom that. "I'm sorry, but that's not what Starfire Security does. We're not assassins." *At least I'm not, not any longer.*

"But you want to be!" Wilsom growled. "I can see the desire burning in your eyes. Consider it a side job beyond your official duties."

Adam shook his head. "Even if I wanted to, as I said, you have no credits. I may be really pissed at Dracu, but I'm not about to risk my life for nothing."

"Once I am installed as the new President, I will have access to the planetary treasury. I will pay you a *million* energy credits if you help me. And you need not do it alone; I will help. I may not have the skills of *The Human*, but I am an asset."

Indo and the others were listening, tension on their faces, waiting to hear what Adam would say. A million *friggin'* credits....

Wilsom looked at the others. "And your team may join us. I will contribute another half a million for them."

Indo waved his hand and shook his head. "No, thank you! I barely got out of the last mission on Osino with my life. I am not about to go right back in."

The others echoed his sentiment.

Wilsom looked back at Adam. "That will be better! A small team of two. No one will suspect us returning so soon. No elaborate planning or army. Just kill them, and then let me take it from there. My supporters will rally to my side, as we expected them to do this night. They will rejoice in the death of the tyrant and the evil merchant who has been making a fortune off of their suffering. I know you want to do this. Say yes, and I will raise the fee to one and a half million."

"Credits you *don't* have," Adam reiterated.

"However, if you are successful, then I will. It comes down to your confidence in your abilities."

Adam turned to his team.

"Do not look at us," Indo said, still shaking his head. "This is entirely your decision. We are going back to Tel'oran, but for a million and a half credits, we would not blame you for staying on Osino a while longer."

Adam grinned. Damn, how could he say no? Two quick kills, which in reality was much simpler than staging a planet-wide coup. He'd done it before, lots of times. He could almost do it in his sleep. And besides, he owed Dracu Hor a bullet through the head.

"Oh, what the hell," Adam finally said. "It's not like I've never killed an alien before. Besides, these guys deserve it. Okay, Wilsom, you've just hired yourself an assassin."

## 4

The transport starship was called the CX-91, and after the team boarded the vessel, it was pulled away from Osino and hidden in the outer system while another Starfire craft was brought in from a nearby system to take the remainder of Adam's team back to headquarters. The delay gave Adam time to work up a plan for assassinating two targets with only one shooter.

It wouldn't be easy, not because of the targets, but because he had to dispatch both of them at essentially the same time. Otherwise, there was a chance one would learn of the assassination of the other and go to ground, locking themselves away in a bunker somewhere until the threat passed. And Adam didn't want to have any collateral damage, such as would be present with a bomb large enough to take out the Presidential Palace when both Creel and Dracu were there. Adam smirked at the thought. Collateral damage was kind of his signature. If you hired *The Human*, you had to factor in at least some widespread havoc. But Adam had no beef with the Osino population beyond that of the President and Dracu Hor. He had to be careful that helping install Wilsom as the new president didn't come at too high of a price.

Another factor was the timing. Wilsom was right: No one would be expecting such action so soon after the failed insurrection. Even then, the *purges* were beginning. Local newscasts monitored from space were full of stories about how Creel had set in motion a deadly cleansing of the population of anyone who supported the revolution. These widescale actions had to be helped along by Dracu, who had an inside track into the rebels and their organization. After all, he was one of them—indeed, he was the instigator. He knew all the names and the locations of their safehouses. This made the purge especially bloody and with it beginning as early as the morning after the failed coup. By noon, two thousand people had been arrested, with another one hundred deaths in violent altercations with the authorities. And the momentum was only growing stronger.

"Here, see if these fit," Adam said to Wilsom on the third day on the starship. He handed him some of Span's old clothes. His now-deceased teammate and the Osinolese were about the same size, and Span's outfits were similar to what the natives wore.

"What is this for?" Wilsom growled. He was upset with Adam that they hadn't already transitioned back to the surface. He was itching for some action, thinking every day in space was another day for Dracu and Creel to consolidate their power. It also meant more deaths of his followers.

"I need you to make a series of recordings, each in different outfits, to make it look as if you made them over time," Adam explained. "We'll send them to the surface to make Dracu believe you are still off-planet. Make them rousing, patriotic speeches, encouraging your people to stand strong. We don't want our enemy to even suspect you're back on the surface."

"So, when do we go back to Osino?"

"Five days. I have another Starfire ship being brought in from a system about five hundred light-years from here where another team was doing an operation. My people will catch a ride with them back to Tel'oran."

"That is good. I have a plan—"

"Planning is my job," Adam interrupted.

"But I know Creel's routine."

"I just spent two months studying his movements as closely as anyone, and from a tactical vantage, as well. And Dracu, we've been working with him daily for all that time. I already have a plan."

"What is it?"

"I prefer to keep that to myself."

"In case I get caught?"

Adam laughed. "Dude, if you get caught, all bets are off. That means you won't have the money to pay me. In that case, I'm gone. No pay, no play, as we Humans say."

Although the two had been joined at the hip for the past two months, Wilsom still hadn't fully acclimated to Human-speak. Even so, he got the gist of the comment. He even managed a smile.

"In that case, you will have to rescue me ... if you wish to get paid. But in all seriousness, I have devised a plan I think will work."

"And how many heavily guarded public figures have *you* assassinated in the past?"

"I return the question to you. How many have *you*?"

Adam stared evenly at the alien, a slight grin on his face. He didn't say anything, letting the mysterious reputation of *The Human* do the speaking for him.

"Very well," said Wilsom. "We will go with your unspoken plan first."

Adam nodded. "Now, let's get you making the broadcasts. While you're doing that, I'll be collecting the equipment I'll need."

Five days later, Indo Sahir's green-tinted forehead was creased with concern as he stood with Adam, about to enter the umbilical tube to board the second Starfire ship.

"There will be no one to back you up should something go wrong," he said.

Adam smiled. "Hey, what could go wrong?"

Indo didn't take the bait. He pursed his lips and shook his head. "Flippant to the end."

"This isn't the end. And don't worry; I have a plan."

"We also had a plan to replace Creel. You see how well that worked out."

"I know more about the players involved than we did before. I won't be so trusting this time around."

"I wish you luck, my friend." They made a traditional Human handshake, something Adam had instituted among Starfire personnel. "Make quick work of this and get back to Tel'oran as soon as possible. I will worry until I hear word of your departure from this cesspool of a planet. This place is not worth losing your life over."

"Thank you for that. I'll do my best not to let you down."

And then Indo was gone.

The CX-91 was in orbit around the fifth planet in the star system and would be relatively safe while Adam and Wilsom journeyed back to Osino in the shuttle. As such a minor world with a small population and a single export crop, there wasn't a lot of traffic throughout the rest of the system. It also made landing on the planet in secret a piece of cake since there was no extensive planetary traffic control system.

The pair of conspirators wouldn't be landing near Shore's End; however, they would be going to a neighboring city about fifty miles away called Shallows. As the name suggested, it was along the coast and situated on a wide bay with a continental shelf that ran out two hundred miles from the shore. The water here seldom reached a depth of more than fifty feet and was dotted with a myriad of coral islands and alien mangrove swamps. According to Wilsom, he had a loyal cell entrenched in the community. This was the first Adam had heard about the cell, which he said he'd also kept secret from Dracu. Whether it was still intact remained to be seen. No communications would be attempted until they got into town.

The first of the broadcasts were sent out from the CX-91, with Wilsom extolling his people for their bravery and tenacity and promising that he would return soon to help lead them from Creel's tyranny. It was decided not to draw too much attention to Dracu. There was a good chance the general populace wasn't aware of his part in the recent uprising and his subsequent betrayal. Adam wanted him to believe he was flying under the radar and, therefore, would have no need for elaborate security around him.

Adam landed the small shuttlecraft in the water near one of the coral atolls. The great thing about starships is they were also waterproof, and after dislodging the two passengers on dry land, Adam remotely sank the ship below the surface and under a canopy of thick mangrove plants.

Adam carried two large duffle bags, while Wilsom had a smaller pack of clothing and other personal items for Adam. Wilson had come aboard the CX-91 with nothing, and so he had nothing of his own to carry. Adam figured the native would get everything he needed from his friends in the city.

They arrived at dusk and then followed a series of wooden pathways and short bridges between the islands before reaching the mainland. There were three huge Soak Fields for the algae in the bay, which is where most of Shallows residents worked. Although Wilsom wasn't born in the town, he did spend much of his youth there, also working the fields before eventually joining the local police force and then later, President Creel's security detail. Many of the members of his underground cell were friends from his youth. He told Adam he trusted them implicitly. Adam could read the concern on his face for their safety. Had they already been caught up in the purge? They would know soon enough.

Their destination was a small cluster of housing to the south of the city. One of Wilsom's best friends lived there. Fortunately, he had a lot of friends, so it would be hard to identify this one out of the hundreds of others.

At the corner of the house, Adam blended with the shadows and set his bags on the ground, hiding them under a large, tropical bush. He carried dual MK-Hybrid handguns on his waist, weapons that featured both a flash component and a ballistic capacity. They were unique, something he fashioned himself. As a Human, he preferred ballistic weapons over bolt launchers for their penetrating power and longer range. But in the alien world, flash bolts worked fine ninety percent of the time. They were great at close range, and the weapons could be recharged countless times or have a new battery snapped into place in seconds. Still, when it came to sheer killing power, nothing beat a lead slug rifling down a six-inch barrel. And the sound it made was music to the Human's ears.

Wilsom moved to the back of the house and peered in a window. There were lights on inside and the smell of food cooking. Adam smirked. Although the city was powered by local cold-fusion reactors, the citizenry still preferred to cook their food the old-fashioned way, with open flames or heated ovens rather than the ubiquitous and sterile food processors. Adam's stomach growled, although he already knew a lot of Osinolese food was incompatible with his Human biology. He brought a small supply of food bars with him, making Wilsom question how long Adam expected the operation to last.

Adam had an answer. "Not long. If it goes out more than a few days, it's because something went wrong."

"Then we try my plan."

"We'll see."

Adam didn't like having his plans questioned or usurped, especially by a rookie like Wilsom. Besides, the native would not have approved of the plan if he had known it ahead of time.

---

Wilsom tapped on the glass, a distinctive three raps, then one, then three again. He then ducked back into the shadows and waited.

A few seconds later, the back door opened, and a thin alien male with three prominent horns on his forehead looked out into the gloom.

"Is someone there?" he whispered. Since there were no indigenous Osinoleses, the population was made up of a menagerie of species. Adam had no idea what this one was called, but the horns were pretty cool.

Wilsom stepped into the light. The reaction from

the horned alien was instantaneous and welcoming. He rushed out and clasped Wilsom's outstretched forearms.

"We saw your broadcast; we thought you were in space!"

"That was the purpose," Wilsom said with a smile. "Are you secure?"

The smile vanished from the friend's face. "For now. There have been many meetings. We are devising contingency plans should Creel's forces close in. But let us not talk out here. The others will be excited to know you have returned."

Adam stepped out of the shadows, drawing an immediate inhale from the friend and a narrowing of his yellow eyes. The thing literally growled at Adam.

"This is my friend," Wilsom said quickly. "He is the one who brought me back to the surface. His name is Bourne, Jason Bourne. This is my friend Hyico."

Adam nodded a noncommittal greeting.

Beforehand, Adam gave Wilsom the cover story he wanted him to use for the Human. His friends were not to know who he was or what his involvement had been in the coup.

"We were betrayed," Wilsom said as the trio moved indoors. "It was Dracu Hor."

"Dracu, the merchant, and now the Vice-President? What does he have to do with the revolution?"

For the duration of the original coup, Dracu had

remained anonymous, preferring to let Wilsom and his notoriety take the spotlight. It allowed the algae exporter to continue to move within the circles of power and provide intelligence to the rebels.

Before Wilsom could explain, three other people joined them in the central room of the home, two males and a female. The males were of different species, but the female had horns of her own, the same as Wilsom's friend. Introductions were made.

"What are your plans now that you are back?" asked the female. Her name was Riggie or something like that. Adam wasn't paying too close attention.

"I will seek to rebuild," Wilsom began. This, too, was part of the cover story. The fewer people who knew of Adam's intentions, the better. "With the purges, it will only cause more anger among the population. We have broached the subject. Now the people know there is a movement afoot to displace the President."

"It will not be easy," said one of the other males. Adam didn't even try to recall his name. He wore a red shirt so he wasn't part of the main story. "So many of our followers have either been arrested, or they are dead. There is much concern for our individual welfare."

"I realize that. It will take time. I plan to move inland to a place where I can move freer. The purges cannot last long. There is too great a need for workers."

Riggie laughed. "That will not be a problem. There was a decree released three days ago that says all rebels captured will be put to work in the Soak Fields immediately and without compensation. These are mostly people who already work there, but now the labor will be had at no cost. And the more they arrest, the more free labor they will have. There are no tribunals, only sentencing. Many are disavowing any loyalty they may have once had to you, so they can keep working for pay to support their families. It appears that will not matter. Creel is only after the free labor at this point."

That was fast, Adam thought. It had only been eight days since the failed revolution. This concern for cheap labor sounded like something Dracu would have pushed with the President. And now, as VP, he had the power to implement the policy. It sounded a lot like the Soviet Gulags or the labor camps of Nazi Germany back on Earth. If you need a labor force, go arrest one.

The rest of the evening was spent with Wilsom detailing Dracu's betrayal. There was to be no mention of an assassination attempt. But soon, sleep overtook the rebel cell, and everyone retired to their quarters. Wilsom was given a spare room while Adam slept on a couch. It had been told that Adam would be leaving in the morning to return to his ship. He was up early the next morning, preparing to leave.

Wilsom met him at the back door. "We will meet later as agreed upon. Together we will make the trip to Shore's End. I will borrow a transport from Hyico."

"Good. I'm going to check on my bags and make sure everything is still in order. You can pick me up on the Coast Road in two hours. Don't be late."

"If I am late, then I am dead."

Adam slipped out the back just as he heard the rumblings of the others in the house as they began their day. There was a thick grove of palm-like trees in the back that was open to a rough field of waist-high bushes and the occasional larger tree. The night before, Adam hid his bags under one of these bushes about fifty yards from the back of the house.

And then he ducked for cover.

To his left were two uniformed soldiers, both of different species, as was common on Osino. They were members of the President's Guard. Hugging the ground, Adam watched them move by and followed quickly by five more. Then he glanced toward the house. There were a couple of dozen additional soldiers closing on the structure.

Once the Guards had passed him, Adam slid in closer to the back of the house. He got there just as the raid took place.

Adam didn't see any weapons in the home the

night before, so there was no counterattack. The soldiers simply swept in and took everyone in custody. And that's when they made a big deal of things, turning on flashing lights and flooding the street and the yard with nearly a hundred soldiers. The President intended to make a spectacle of arresting the infamous revolutionary, Wilsom Panasin.

Adam hid in a bush and watched the back of the house. Wilsom was there, in shackles and being dragged out the door. He looked to the woods, knowing Adam was out there somewhere. Then their eyes met.

Adam grinned and shrugged while Wilsom's jaw tightened. *The Human* waved goodbye.

He'd warned the rebel: *No pay, no play*. And with no chance of Wilsom having access to the planetary treasury, Adam wasn't about to risk his life for nothing. The look on Wilsom's face told Adam he understood. He didn't like it, but what could he do?

A moment later, the early morning quiet returned as Wilsom and his co-conspirators were driven away in armored transports back to Shore's End and a rendezvous with the President and, more than likely, the traitor Dracu Hor.

# 5

The ride into Shore's End was tension-filled as Wilsom stared back at the half dozen soldiers in the transport with him. He knew them all, even to the point where he knew two of them were sympathetic to his cause. They had spent many an hour also complaining about the President's actions. But rather than join Wilsom's revolution, they stayed with Creel. The others were diehard Creel fanatics, so the others dared not speak or show any concern for their prisoner.

Wilsom's anger only grew the closer he got to the Palace. His rebellion had failed utterly, while a person he once considered a friend and confidant betrayed him spectacularly. And now, even *The Human* had abandoned him without so much as lifting a finger to help him. Of the three events, Adam Cain's actions made the most sense, but Wilsom wouldn't admit that. He preferred to remain angry ... at everyone.

And now, only hours after returning to Osino, he had been betrayed yet again as his location was revealed. What had happened to loyalty to a cause? Where were all his friends and supporters?

He was driven through the gates of the Presidential Compound, a place he knew well and only a few short days ago envisioned he would be occupying—as the new President of Osino. He was still to occupy it, but not at the same location as he once imagined. He was to be locked in the cells below the main storerooms, not even under the Palace. That would have been too offensive, with the smell of the desperate and condemned permeating the spaces above. He didn't fear for his life or even the threat of torture. No, he would be kept alive for months—maybe even years— as a show of authority by Creel and, later, Dracu. It was just that he would never see the light of day again beyond today.

When the back door swung open, letting in the harsh light of reality, President Esson Creel was there, along with the turncoat Dracu Hoi. Creel was a tall, stocky and imposing figure, priding himself on his physical presence and conditioning. He exercised near constantly and carried his vanity to the flamboyant and expensive clothing he wore. Dracu shared his taste in fashion, if not his love of exercising.

Dracu was a rotund, yellow-skinned creature with bad teeth.

Creel was shaking his head as Wilsom was placed before him. "My friend, why have you let it come to this?" The President was the consummate politician, a skill that allowed him to gain such high status on Osino in a relatively short time. It was a testament to his glibness and powers of persuasion that an outsider such as he was elected President of the diverse population of the planet. At one time, he and Wilsom had been friends, confidants in a way. They spent hours discussing their vision for the planet, and that was where the divergence began. Soon, it was too much for either of them to bear. If Wilsom hadn't left, he would have been removed, and with prejudice.

"It was you, Esson, who let it come to this. I thought you agreed with my vision?"

"I did, at one time. But times change; my desires change. And that is why our friend Dracu will soon be assuming the role of President. I have achieved about as much as I can expect here on Osino. With the fabulous wealth I have accumulated, I must find a more lavish and accommodating locale to spend my remaining years and away from all these offensive aliens." He waved a hand back at the Presidential Palace. It wasn't much of a palace, just a large home, and not even the largest on Osino. Dracu's home was larger. "I have experienced the best this planet has to offer, and I find it lacking. It is time for me to move on to new challenges, new conquests." He reached out a hand and rested it on Dracu's rounded shoulder. "But seeing that *you*, Wilsom, are not here to replace me—by agreement or by force—then I will leave the planet in Dracu's capable hands. I am sure you will find him a tolerant and benevolent overseer of your long-term imprisonment."

Dracu didn't appear amused by the President's light banter with the prisoner. "Where is *The Human*?" he demanded. "Cain is the only one who would have brought you back to Osino. What are his plans?"

"He has left," Wilsom spat out. "He—like so many of you—has no pride, no loyalty. You only follow the credits."

Dracu laughed. "And you have none, credits, that is. Then his actions are understandable. *The Human* and I understand each other better. We are both professionals, and we know the galaxy runs on credits. Without them, nothing would happen. I am relieved to hear he has left. In many ways, I liked him ... more than I have ever liked you."

Wilsom spit in his face. It was the only act of defiance still open to the rebel.

It was answered by a solid hit to his jaw, being much more powerful than Wilsom would have expected from the merchant. Even so, he got a modicum of satisfaction watching the obese traitor rub his injured wrist as Wilsom was led away.

---

"Then this ends it?" Creel asked his Vice-President as they stood in the morning sunlight.

"Let us hope so. My concern had been *The Human*. Knowing that he is gone is a relief. I know most of Wilsom's forces, and within days, they will be of no concern. And by then, we will have a whole new and inexpensive harvesting cadre which will only make our operations going forward more profitable."

Creel's dark eyes now bore into Dracu's. All pretense of political contriteness was gone. "I am pleased to see that you have so quickly appropriated that which is *mine* and made it *ours*. However, you must exercise patience. The time when this is all yours, and not mine, is not here yet. I still recall that you initiated the rebellion against me. The fact that I have brought you into the fold does not diminish that truth. I made you my Vice-President because I would rather negotiate my way out of an issue rather than fight my way out. That is what Wilsom could never do. But you and I are much alike. You could see the benefit of a peaceful transfer of power rather than setting a precedent for future regime changes. That is to your credit. But remember, the transfer has not yet taken place.

And the timing for such a transfer is up to me if the transfer is to take place at all."

Dracu fought to maintain his composure. He understood what the President was saying. He was not a child needing to be lectured. In fact, Dracu was an experienced merchant and broker, having traveled throughout most of the Sector and beyond. He knew of Creel's background, so he knew himself to be more broadly traveled. He resented the tone the upstart politician used on him.

But he wasn't about to express that to his face.

"Forgive me, my President. It is just that I feel such a bond between us and our joint goals that I naturally ascribe them as *'our'* goals. Of course, you are the President, and you will remain so as long as you wish. Just let it be known that you have a true partner in me, one who shares your vision for Osino and for your future beyond the planet."

"I am confident that you are a partner … at least for the last part of your soliloquy." Then Creel smiled and once again placed his hand upon Dracu's shoulder. "Believe me when I say that the sooner I make my departure from this backward waste-hole of a world, the happier I will be. So, please, do not do anything that will upset my plans. That would make me very angry."

Dracu excused himself from the President's presence shortly after that, afraid his temper might get the best of him. Then with two security personnel in attendance, he enjoyed the drive back to his estate in the hills east of Shore's End.

His relationship with Creel was a strange affair. Most times, they tolerated each other. On rare occasions, they actually got along. But he had to put away his animosities toward the politician and focus on the here and now. His time would come to rule Osino. He had waited this long. He could wait another two years.

But now he could relax, possibly even celebrate. Since the beginning of the chain of events that led him to betray the revolution, his main concern had been the reactions of *The Human*, Adam Cain. Dracu had sincerely hoped that Cain would have been killed in the attack the other night. But as he said to the Human at the time, he was pretty sure he would survive. After all, Humans had an uncanny ability to do just that, even against the worst of odds.

And now—if Wilsom was to be believed—Cain had returned the rebel to the planet but then quickly retreated once Wilsom was arrested. It made sense that he would. His loyalty was to the credits for a job and not the job itself. But the fact that he was still working with Wilsom up until the arrest bothered him. Obviously, he was promised credits. That was what beings like him lived for. In that regard, Dracu and Cain were much alike.

And yet Dracu had betrayed him. That was the unknown in the equation.

Dracu then shook his head. *That is wrong,* he thought. *I did not betray Cain; I betrayed Wilsom. This is not Cain's war. His involvement began and ended with the exchange of credits.*

Even so, Dracu knew what Wilsom had done. He promised Cain credits from the treasury, payable once he was installed as President. Why else would Cain return? Surely not to seek revenge on Dracu. They had agreed it was only business, not personal. Yes, the Human was angry; that was to be expected. But he was pragmatic. There was no profit in coming after Dracu simply for revenge.

And now that Wilsom was in a dungeon at the Presidential Compound, Dracu didn't have much to worry about. He would let Creel be the face of the purges while he continued to whisper in the President's ear. But Creel was shrewd. Dracu would have to be careful with him, continually playing on the President's plans to move on from the backward waste-hole of Osino.

Yes, Osino was a waste-hole. But it would soon be Dracu's waste-hole.

## 6

Dracu had a lavish home built and paid for by his lucrative near monopoly on the export trade of the Salvish Algae. He shared the export rights with two other brokers, with each sharing equal portions of the trade. This was something instituted by President Creel immediately after he came to power six years before. It was a masterful tactic on his part, splitting the trade among only three. Each would make a substantial profit while at the same time making it impossible for any of them to merge with the other to form a stronger bloc. There would only be three, and there would *always* be three. Merge if you like, but then two would share in only one-third of the trade.

Even so, the credits were incredible as the bio-engineered algae became the go-to ingredient for countless products. In a galaxy replete with star travel, minerals, metals and precious gems were plentiful, found on myriad asteroids and uninhabited worlds. There was little profit to be found in such products. But organic material, that which had to be grown or could only be grown in certain environments, was where the credits lie. And after the disruption caused by the Klin invasion, most of the traditional commodity coalitions had broken down. This allowed others to enter a market that had long since been cornered by other interests. Dracu saw his opportunity and was lucky enough to be one of the three chosen to represent Salvish Algae. And once he became President, he would do away with the other two exporters and control all the trade. After that, Dracu had no idea what he would do. But he would have all the credits he needed to do ... anything he wished.

---

Dracu lived alone in the large home, the same home that months ago had hosted a rebel named Wilsom and a Human name Cain. Here they planned the coup.

Now, it was a place of solitude, of peace. Dracu poured an intoxicant. He would partake, then partake some more. He had very little to do beyond wait for the planet to be given to him.

He laid back on a soft, imported sofa, bathed in the diffused light coming in through the treated glass of the expansive patio doors. A gentle breeze circulated through the room, carrying with it the fragrance of the purple blooms of the *cranish* flowers in the garden. He closed his eyes, letting the warmth of the intoxicant flow through him.

Then he frowned. He opened his eyes and cocked his head toward the patio doors. He could not remember leaving them open. Perhaps one of the guards had done so....

He lifted his glass to take another swig, and as he did, he caught a movement behind him reflected in the ice within the glass.

His reactions weren't even close enough to stop the powerful forearm from wrapping around his neck and pulling him over the back of the sofa. Dracu wasn't used to physical violence; his wrist still hurt from when he hit Wilsom earlier. But even if he were, it would not have mattered. Dracu Hor was on the floor and staring into the laughing blue eyes of *The Human*, Adam Cain.

---

"I thought we had an understanding," Dracu pleaded, his eyes darting to and fro, hoping to see his bodyguards enter and with weapons flashing.

"Sorry, Dracu, but your bodyguards are otherwise

occupied. In Human-speak, that means they're dead. And as far as an understanding ... that we did have. I thought you understood that I was going to kill you someday."

"That is *not* what I understood. You were not to hold a *grudge*, as was translated."

"Well, sorry about that. I should have made my message clearer. But even if I didn't, you should have known better. I don't like to be betrayed; who does?"

"I apologize! Sincerely, I do. But there has been no harm. As I said, your company has been paid, and you survive. Why risk your life coming back? And with Wilsom in custody, there is no chance of him paying you unless you intend to free him! Are you insane ... forgive me; I mean not to insult!"

Adam was enjoying the hell out of this. Normally, he wasn't a cruel man. Not normally. But stab him in the back, and all bets were off. This was now a matter of pride.

"No, Wilsom can stay where he is. I'm not interested in freeing him."

"Then what *are* your intentions? Are you here to kill me?"

Adam watched the relief flow over Dracu's face when Adam shook his head and pursed his lips. "Nah, I'm not going to kill you. But we *are* going to take a ride."

# 7

Adam had 'borrowed' a transport from the city of Shallows earlier that morning and driven it to Shore's End. Now, he had Dracu drive them back into the city and to the town center with its iconic watchtower lording over everything. Most of the town had been affected in one way or another by the battle that took place here eight nights ago, and with no effort made to date to begin the cleanup. People were still in too much shock over what happened. There were destroyed buildings, blown up half-tracks and even a few half-eaten bodies still scattered about, waiting to be removed. Essentially, Shore's End was nearly deserted, which suited Adam's plan to a 't.'

They parked at the base of the four-hundred-foot-tall structure. Dracu was old and overweight and no match for the Human, and he knew it. Besides, Adam had his ubiquitous double hybrid weapons carried in holsters around his waist. Telling the merchant that Adam wasn't going to kill him brought with it a level of cooperation, so much so that Dracu helped Adam carry one of his bags to the top of the tower.

Climbing the two hundred twenty-nine steps was a chore for the native, taking a full twenty minutes to do the climb when counting the rest breaks. Dracu asked Adam several times what he was planning, with each inquiry met with silence. After a while, the alien gave up. But now that they were at the top of the tower, Dracu began to suspect the truth. His suspicions were confirmed when Adam withdrew the four-foot-long barrel of his K-9 sniper rifle and began assembling the rest of the weapon.

"You intend to shoot Creel!" he said, aghast.

"I do," was all he said. And then Adam watched a change come over Dracu. It was almost laughable, as the algae merchant saw his opportunity to assume the President's position sooner rather than later. After that, Dracu couldn't do enough to help Adam set up his equipment.

The Presidential Compound was in clear view from the crow's nest, something Adam always found disturbing. Why wasn't the tower manned around the clock by Creel's Guards? Or why wasn't it either dismantled or at least secured better than it was? It had a commanding view of the front of the Palace and was, therefore, a major security risk. But Adam wasn't about to look a gift horse in the mouth.

Adam and his team had studied Creel's movements extensively prior to the night assault on the Compound. They knew how often he would leave the building and the routines he followed religiously. Having such a predictable lifestyle was not wise for any high-profile celebrity; it almost invited an attempt on their life. But Creel was secure in his hold over the people of Osino, at least until Wilson resigned, giving a face to the unrest that was rapidly building.

"I must admire the skill it will take to hit a target at this distance," Dracu was saying. "And these weapons, these are of Human design, are they not?"

"That's right," Adam said, opening up a little more to talk about one of his favorite rifles. "It's a Browning K9 Long Distance Sniper Rifle. It fires a 7.62 open tip matched, 175-grain round. The effective range is over three thousand yards." Adam took out a range finder and measured the distance to the front of the palace. "We're only looking at a little over six hundred yards. And thanks to the miracle of modern alien technology, I have a customized targeting computer that will accurately measure wind speed, humidity, local gravity and even the rotation of the planet. I'll be able to dial this in five-by-five."

"Five-by-five?"

"With clarity and accuracy. Once locked in, even *you* could make the shot."

Dracu laughed nervously. Adam could tell he was beginning to wonder what he was up here for, and it surely wasn't to help him carry his bags.

"Now, Dracu, you may open the bag you carried up here."

With the slightest hesitation, Dracu unzipped the bag. Inside were clothing and a tactical helmet like the ones Adam's team wore the night of the attack.

"Put them on; they should fit, although I had to guess your size. The uniform belonged to Span. You remember him, one of my team members. He's dead now, by the way, killed by one of your fucking Spiders."

Dracu's normally yellow skin turned about three shades lighter as he suddenly realized there was nothing magnanimous about Adam's treatment of him. Something horrific was about to happen, and Dracu was powerless to stop it.

"Why do you want me in this clothing?" he mustered the courage to ask.

"Nothing to worry about," Adam said. "It's just for show, part of the act." Adam rested his hand on the grip of one of his MK-Hybrids. "Now, do as I say. It's getting late, and there's still so much to do."

It was nearing four in the afternoon, and President Esson Creel was feeling giddy. His day had gone well, first with the capture of his arch-nemesis, Wilsom Panasin, and now with the confirmation that another thousand natives had been swept up in the purge and would soon be back in the fields working diligently harvesting the algae, but this time working for free. Of course, it still meant Creel would have to drastically increase the size of the makeshift prison yard he was building in the burnt-out section of forest south of the city. The fires wrought by the gangly metal tanks called Spiders had effectively cleared the ground, allowing for the conscripted laborers to also set to work building their own cage. Spiked wire barriers were going up, with canvas tents serving as temporary shelters. Fortunately, this was the temperate time of the year in Shore's End, so the tents would do just fine for now.

Creel snickered. At the pace things were going, he may not even be here when the weather shifted. It rarely snowed along the shore, but it did get cold. With the accelerated profits this new workforce could bring him, he could reach his goal in credits sooner than two years from now; at which point, he would turn it all over the ambitious Dracu Hor. Although Dracu was older than Creel, he still had the lust for power that Creel once had. Perhaps having achieved it already was the reason he no longer considered power the pinnacle of his ambitions. Now, he sought only creature comforts and the kind only credits could buy. And if he were to truly enjoy the benefits of wealth, he preferred to do it sharing the company of those of his own species. Aliens were such disgusting creatures, and he had lived among them for over twenty years. Enough was enough. Besides, he was tired of playing god on this stinking world, which constantly smelled of rotting fish and equally rotting algae. As he worked the numbers out in his head, he reached the conclusion that he would indeed have enough credits to retire by the time the cold north winds began to blow. That would make Dracu happy. Rather than two years away, it was only four months, and the sickly and overweight merchant could have it all. And good riddance.

Creel looked at the clock on the wall. It was time for his afternoon walk. The President prided himself on his superb physical conditioning, and he stayed true to his exercise regime every day possible. However, for the past week or so, he had forgone his walks because of the unrest in the area. He had a track within the Palace, yet he preferred the feel of sunshine on his tanned face and the air from outside, even if it did smell of dead fish and algae. But now that Wilsom was in custody and *The Human* was gone, Creel allowed himself time to relax and restart his favored exercise routine.

He left his work desk and went to the door to his

office, where he nearly collided with his panicking Chief of Staff, Alacot Lassidor.

"No, my President! You cannot go outside."

"What is the issue?" Creel took the warning seriously, considering all that had taken place over the past eight days.

"A report has been received of an assassin within the watchtower. I have sent Guards to investigate. As you know, the landmark has a clear view of the Compound."

Creel bit his bottom lip. *Yes, it does,* he thought acidly. Years before, he had advocated for its removal, and this very same Chief of Staff had convinced him otherwise, seeing that the tower was an ancient landmark, over two hundred years old and the symbol of Shore's End. This was right after Creel came to power, and he wasn't anxious to upset the natives. Since that time, he had failed to revisit the topic of the watchtower's removal. Perhaps this was now the time.

His Chief of Staff was on a link with the troops on the ground, relaying the running commentary to the president.

"They are making entry. No resistance. They are on the stairs." A few minutes later: "Preparing to breach the top floor. There is yelling … and flash bolts. Yes, a subject has been killed." A slight hesitation. "He is down. There is a sophisticated ballistic weapon on site." He looked into Creel's eyes. "It appears to be of Human design."

"And he is dead?"

His assistant nodded emphatically. "Yes. Confirmed."

Creel pressed past his Chief of Staff and left the building. Stepping out into the late afternoon sun, he looked sharply to the south and the tower off in the distance. It was too far away for him to make out any details in the crow's nest, although he did see an occasional reflection off metal as the sun angled toward the sea. His troops were there, securing the site. This was indeed a glorious day. First Wilsom, and now *The Human*....

"My President!" Alacot cried out as he exited the building. "Our troops have removed the helmet worn by the assassin. It was not *The Human*. It was Dracu Hor. Dracu was the assassin—wait, there is more."

Creel stood impatient as someone was talking in Alacot's ear. During the lull, he attempted to absorb the information he'd just been told. Had Dracu intended to assassinate him just so he could become President sooner? That was a foolish and dangerous escalation. It had only been a few weeks since Creel offered the Vice-Presidency to the merchant in the first place. Was he that impatient that he could not wait? But he *did* initiate a coup against Creel. Dracu was indeed a reckless and unstable creature. Then he snorted. What a reckless and unstable creature Dracu *had been* was now correct. He was dead, a victim of his own impatience and lust for power. How his death complicated Creel's future plans, he was uncertain.

Alacot now turned to Creel, his eyes wide, his mouth hanging slack. "What is the issue?" Creel asked.

"My President, Dracu was taped to the weapon, secured there to make it look as if he was about to shoot. He wore a helmet, the same as the Human's team of mercenaries wore the night of the raid. Under it, his mouth was gagged. Dracu was not the assassin. He was a victim."

"He was not?" Creel looked again at the distant tower. "If he was not the assassin, then who is? And if not in the tower, then where?"

Creel suddenly twisted his head, looking north to the small rise in the distance that could be seen over the surrounding wall. As with the watchtower, it, too, had a clear view of the front of the Palace, if at a greater distance.

---

Alacot didn't know what brought the sudden shower of liquid to his face; the sky was clear, and no rain was forecast. And then he noticed the color on his shirt and hands. It was red. And then President Creel fell into him. Alacot caught him, keeping them both from falling to the ground. Alacot then dropped to his knees, cradling the President's head in his hands. The eyes were open but vacant, and there was a neat hole just above his left eye with a trickle of blood flowing from it. And then Alacot's hand felt the back of Creel's head —what there was left of it. All he found was a jagged cavity where the skull once was. The killing wound was the source of all the blood and sinew that now covered the Chief of Staff.

Alacot looked around, and it was only then that he heard the distant echo of a soft explosion. It came from the north, upon the ridge where Creel had been looking. It was from there that the assassin took his shot.

Confused and frightened, Alacot discarded the carcass of the former President and crawled for cover behind a nearby transport. Was the killer still searching for targets, looking to take out any of the ranking staff of the President? Alacot was as high as they came, with the exception of ... Dracu Hor!

Both the President and Vice-President were dead, making these actions related and a concerted effort on the part of the rebels. They had not been defeated the other night as had been suspected, nor during the violent purges of the past few days. They were still strong and able and with their leader locked in a dungeon only a few hundred feet from where Alacot cowered.

Guards were running in all directions, armed yet with no target in sight. Alacot wanted to tell them to access the grassy knoll to the north, but then he hesitated. What if the Guards were part of Wilsom's cadre? If not all, then some. Were they waiting for this moment to reveal themselves and join in the coup?

Being the survivalist that he was, Alacot made a decision. Gaining as much courage as his weakened knees could muster, he rose from behind the transport, confident that Creel had been the assassin's only target. He now moved to the bank of storage buildings and through the door that led down to the dungeons. Both in the yard and in the buildings, Guards were in a panic. Bolts were being launched, not from outside the Compound but from inside. These would be hidden rebel sympathizers facing off against Creel's loyalists. But Creel was dead, so there was nothing for which the loyalists to fight.

This gave Alacot the confidence he needed to do what he intended. At the door to Wilsom's cell, he placed the key he carried as the Chief of Staff and set the rebel free, the person who was now the de facto leader of the planet Osino.

Perhaps Wilsom Panasin will be looking for a competent Chief of Staff. If so, then Alacot would surely petition for the position. Setting him free would go a long way in helping the new President make his selection.

## 8

Adam continued scanning the Compound through the rifle's scope, seeing the chaos and the occasional flash of bolt launches. He suspected the fighting wouldn't last long. During the research for the coup, he learned the Guards were not a loyal group, at least not to an individual. For the most part, they respected the office of the President more than they did the person occupying it. Still, some were expressing their displeasure that Creel was dead. But at this point, there was no end game, no point in their protests.

Even so, Adam would give it until tomorrow morning for things to settle down. Wilsom would be free by then and quickly consolidating his power. It would be risky to show up at the Palace door now and proudly claim credit for the assassination. Tomorrow would be better.

Adam loaded his gear in the borrowed transport and drove it further into the northern woods. With most natives being larger than a Human, the vehicle was roomy. He climbed in the backseat and stretched out. He had the forethought to bring a light blanket in his gear, along with water and the food packets. He would spend the night here and then move into town at first light.

---

Adam approached the open gates without his trusty MK-Hybrids strapped around his waist. He carried the gear bag but no outright weapons that might spook someone.

The Compound was a beehive of activity even at this early hour. There were still plenty of guards around, but they didn't seem as agitated as yesterday afternoon. These were the survivors, the ones who stuck around after Creel was killed. They all knew Wilsom, so, hopefully, it had been a relatively peaceful transition of power.

None of the Guards knew who he was, but with so many newcomers coming and going, they didn't pay him much attention. Adam grimaced. If he were seeking more income from the new leader, he would recommend a complete overhaul of the security protocols for the site, with the first order of business being the dismantling of the watchtower and a taller wall to the north.

Eventually, his presence was challenged, and he was laughed at when he said he was here to see the new president. The attitude changed when he said to tell him that *The Human* was here. Few of the Guards had heard of him in his capacity as an Indie, but they had all heard of the Human race. What he was doing here, and at this critical time, was enough for a runner to be sent to the Palace.

The reaction was immediate. Wilsom himself raced from the building and walked quickly up to Adam. His expression was one of anger; his reaction at being locked up yesterday could have gone either way. Wilsom chose anger.

"It was you who informed on me, was it not?" he accused.

The Guards lifted their Xan-fis, seeing the anger directed at the new arrival.

"It seemed like the best way to get Creel to let down his guard and to keep you safe."

"Safe! He could have killed me."

"That wasn't going to happen."

"Says you from your vast experience at organizing coups?"

"Something like that. Well, were you tortured … or killed."

"Of course, I was not. But I would have preferred to be informed as to your plan. I was in despair, believing all was lost."

"It had to look convincing."

Wilsom looked to the tower. "And it had been your plan all along to use Dracu as a distraction?"

"I would have preferred to kill him myself, but this worked out just as well."

Wilsom let his anger fade. What was done was done, and in the end, Adam's plan worked. Wilsom was the new leader of Osino and without Dracu to share in the power.

"Come, my friend," Wilsom said, wrapping an arm around Adam's shoulder. The Guards relaxed, although a squad did accompany the pair to the Palace entrance. A thin, blue-skinned alien holding a datapad watched nervously as they passed through the double entry doors and then followed a few paces behind.

Wilsom looked over his shoulder at the being. "This is Alacot Lassidor, my new Chief of Staff. He has been with Creel since the beginning. He's the one who set me free last night."

Adam didn't acknowledge him; he wasn't here for pleasantries. The Human was here for his million and a half energy credits.

They entered Creel's—now Wilsom's—Presidential office.

"I have been in here more times than I can count, and yet now it feels different." When Adam didn't ask how Wilsom volunteered the answer. "Now, it feels more natural, like it has always been mine. Thanks to you, today marks a new beginning for Osino, a fundamental change from the way things used to be."

Adam pursed his lips, almost tempted to ask what changes Wilsom was about to introduce. But he resisted. Just give him his money, and he'd be headed back to his ship. As it was, Tidus was going to be pissed that Adam took the side job. He was resigned to the fact that a portion of the one-point-five mill would go to the company, even though it wasn't an official Starfire assignment.

"When do I get my money?" Adam asked impatiently, still standing and holding the duffle bag in his left hand.

It took a moment for the translation bug to link the word *money* with *credits*.

"Yes, about that," Wilsom began, which made Adam's stomach tighten. "There is a process with the finance council that must be followed. It seems most of the treasury is held off planet, on Tactori. Esson was co-mingling his funds with those of the planet, and the bankers are sorting through the confusion. In anticipation of your arrival, I began the inquiries this morning.

It should only take a few days before I have full access to the funds."

"A few days? That's not acceptable," Adam said. "I've overstayed my time here as it is."

"Then you are free to go," Wilsom said quickly. "I will send the funds to you as they become available."

Adam winced. "I don't think so. That's not how these things go. We usually get a sizeable deposit or payment in full before the job is started. I trusted you, Wilsom. I need to get paid."

"And that trust will be rewarded. You took on an impossible mission, and you did it on faith. I appreciate that. It is just that—even as President—there are steps that must be taken. I was not aware that Creel kept the bulk of the funds off-world. Continue with your trust for a few more days, and you will be richly rewarded. And in the meantime—" he waved his hand around the room "—you will stay here, in the Palace, and with access to the finest Osino has to offer. We even have food processors that can prepare any meal compatible with Humans."

Wilsom had taken a seat on the other side of a gargantuan desk—the cliche symbol of a tyrannical leader of a no-nothing world. He nodded to his Chief of Staff; Adam didn't remember the name. "Please escort our guest to the finest room the Palace offers, with the exception of the Presidential Suite." Wilsom laughed. "That room is reserved for *me*."

As he was led from the room, Adam sensed a change in Wilsom. He was not the same spirited, even childlike revolutionary he had been over the past two months. Adam had been with him almost around the clock for that time, so he had a pretty good idea what Wilsom was like. Now, he seemed changed, as if seething anger lay just below the surface like a sleeping volcano, to be unleashed at any time. It was understandable. The decision to leave Creel's service and embark on the life of a rebel on the run had to be a tough one. And then the coup and all the disappointment that surrounded it. And then suddenly, here he was, the big fish in a small pond, although he didn't consider Osino a small pond. To Wilsom, he was the King of the World. And in a very real sense, he was.

---

The blue-skinned alien led Adam to a stairway, and they climbed it in silence. The Chief of Staff wore a frown on his forehead that seemed natural, although Adam had no way of knowing for sure. Everyone was under a lot of stress—except for Wilsom. He seemed to be the only person enjoying the moment.

At the top of the stairs, Adam was led to a six-panel door with an ornately carved frame. The room was what one would expect. Creel had inherited the home from the past President and then, over the years, made it his own. He was in the process of turning Osino into a commercial powerhouse built on the green miracle plant. He entertained scientists, financiers and corporate entities from across the galaxy as he petitioned for the exclusive rights to grow Salvish Algae.

If Adam wasn't in such a hurry to get his money and leave, this would have been a pretty nice vacation suite.

"It was you who orchestrated the assassinations of both the President and the Vice-President," the Chief of Staff stated, finally letting his curiosity take over.

"That's right," Adam said. There was no point in keeping it secret any longer. "What do you think of that?"

"It is of no concern to me."

Adam tossed his bag on the huge bed. "No concern of yours? It upset your entire life; the entire power structure of your planet."

"I do a job for my employer, that is all. And I am very good at it. I study, and I advise, but I attempt never to get political. I only want the best for my President, no matter who that might be."

"Even so, you must be relieved to be rid of that tyrant Creel."

"Tyrant, Esson Creel?" The native seemed genuinely surprised. "President Creel was anything but a tyrant."

Adam laughed. "And you said you don't get political."

"I am not; I simply speak the truth."

"What about all the people dying in the Soak Fields?"

"Algae farming is a dangerous business. President Creel is the one who introduced the crop to Osino, bringing us prosperity and introducing our world to the galaxy. He leveraged the exclusive growing rights for the benefit of the people. Of course, there were trials at the beginning as we all learned how to harvest the product. In the beginning, five times as many died. It was through his reforms and innovations that the number is as low as it is now."

"You better not let Wilsom hear you say that. To him, Creel was the devil himself."

"Officer Panasin was the strongest advocate for increasing harvest yields. Once he reached the advisory level with the President, he became very involved in the operation of the fields. I must admit, by that time, the President was losing interest in his position. You must know he was planning on abdicating the title. He chose Dracu to be his successor."

"You say Wilsom wanted *higher* yields? Wouldn't that mean more deaths?"

"Of course. That was the main point of disagreement and the reason why Wilsom was released."

"Released?"

"Told to leave."

"I thought he was the one who quit."

"That is the story that circulated. But I was here at the time. I know what took place." The Chief of Staff now waved his hand and moved to the door. "All of that is in the past. I now serve the new President and will do so with loyalty and efficiency for as long as he needs me. Enjoy your stay. If you need anything, a service bot is at your command."

After the blue-skinned alien left, Adam moved to the double French doors and looked out over the Compound below. He was troubled by what he'd been told, but he tried to keep things in perspective. He was an independent security officer, hired to do whatever job he was paid to do. Very often, he and others of his kind worked both sides of the fence, for the good guys and the bad guys. In the end, it didn't matter. One man's villain was another man's saint. It was all a matter of perspective. So what if Wilsom wasn't the altruistic and caring rebel he made himself out to be? And so what if Creel wasn't as bad a guy as he was told? It was just a job, right? It's not like he killed the wrong guy.

Adam went to his bag and pulled out a small Sig Sauer 9 mm he had as a backup. He placed the weapon in his sock since strapping on dual MK-Hybrids might attract the wrong kind of attention. He felt the need for a little personal protection.

He then spread out on the bed. Sleeping in the car last night was okay, but his back was stiff. And the damn bed was luxurious. *Just hang out here for a couple of days, and everything will be fine*, Adam said to himself. Don't let the politics of the situation bother him. He was a professional. Emotions were not part of the equation.

Even then, Adam continued to stare at the roof, wondering if he had made the right decision backing Wilsom. Then he snorted. A million and a half credits said he made the right call.

# 9

Adam took the first meal in his room, considering it his private sanctuary protected from the politics of the Palace. At least he didn't have to be around the gloating Wilsom Panasin. He was anxious to get paid and off the planet as soon as possible. He even considered making a link with Tidus to tell him he'd be back soon, and with a huge bonus for both of them. By now, his team would have told him what Adam was up to. Tidus had been in the security business for thirty years, first with Priority Acquisitions and now with his own company, Starfire Security. And if there was one thing Adam knew neither company specialized in, it was assassinations. That was taboo. And now Adam had allowed himself to be lured into doing just that. Sure, it was off the books as far as Starfire was concerned. But Adam was *The Human,* and *The Human* was inexorably linked to Starfire. That was intentional. Now Tidus would be regretting that branding.

The more he thought about it, the more Adam came to realize what a shitstorm he had waiting for him back on Tel'oran. And if the truth came out that Wilsom may be worse than the person Adam was hired to assassinate, well, he didn't want to think about that. He had to focus on Dracu. The turncoat had cost the lives of two of Tidus's agents. Getting revenge on him would be something Tidus would welcome. But not the unsanctioned assassination of a planetary head-of-state.

Maybe Wilsom wasn't so bad. Maybe Adam was reading this all wrong.

---

Later in the afternoon, Adam was summoned to Wilsom's office.

"I think you will find this interesting," the former rebel leader said enthusiastically. "Come, join me on the parade field."

Adam was concerned when they stepped outside to find a row of Presidential Guards lined up and being watched by another line of armed soldiers. Adam made a quick count—nineteen.

Wilsom waved a hand at the prisoners.

"These are my former loyalists, friends of mine who had previously expressed support for my cause and actions. And yet rather than join me, they remained with Creel. They did not inform on me, nor did they do any actions that would hinder my movement. And that is their sin."

"What sin?" Adam asked.

"They remained in the service of the former President, even though they despised him. They feigned loyalty while remaining disloyal. How could I ever trust beings like that to serve me?"

"They were loyal to *you*," Adam said in their defense, sensing what was about to happen.

"Or so they say. Knowing how well they deceived Creel, they could just as easily deceive *me*. They have proven as much."

"This is crazy. You're going to kill people who were—are—loyal to you simply because they hid their feelings and kept their jobs. Not everyone has the balls to stand up to a President."

Wilsom was confused by the comment but let it go. He understood enough.

"I find it amusing that *The Human* would show such compassion for creatures he has never met. That is not your reputation. I thought you would understand and respect what I am about to do."

"Hey, it's your planet; do what you want. Just don't do this out of some need to impress me."

Wilsom's jaw tightened, and his eyes burned. "You think I do this to impress *you*? You are gravely mistaken. I do this for me, for all the anguish I've felt, for all the frustration that my vision for Osino was ignored."

"Yeah, I heard about your vision for Osino," Adam growled. "And here I thought Creel was the bastard."

Again, the literal translation of the word *bastard* confused the alien. "I cannot speak to that. But I can and will exercise my rights as the leader of Osino."

He directed his attention to the Guard commander and nodded. A moment later, the Compound was lit by the simultaneous firing of multiple bolt launchers, all at Level-1, and a moment later, Wilsom's nineteen former friends and comrades lay dead and smoldering on the ground.

"Just get me my credits, and I'll be gone," Adam growled.

"As quickly as possible," Wilsom replied with matching venom. Then he turned abruptly and strode back into the Palace without waiting for Adam.

A line had been crossed, and from here on out, Adam had to be extremely careful if he wanted to make it off Osino in one piece.

## 10

Another two days passed without Adam seeing Wilsom or his money coming through. By now, Adam was looking for an exit, a way off the planet that wouldn't cost him his life. To Adam, he was worth a lot more than a mill-and-a-half, and it might be best to write this one off and live to fight another day. But he was ensconced in Wilsom's palace and with hundreds of armed soldiers now completely devoted to his every wish. The slayings in the courtyard the day before had made a profound effect. Everyone was nervous and serious. There was no celebration for the new regime, and from the snippets Adam got from the Chief of Staff—his name was Alacot—Wilsom was becoming more agitated by the minute.

It seemed the purges were continuing, even though

it was now loyalists of Creel's that were being rounded up ... along with Wilsom's rebels. The new President was expressing the same twisted logic he used with the soldiers: If these people would harbor revolutionary feelings against Creel, then they could just as easily feel the same toward him. The new internment camps were overflowing in only a matter of days.

Alacot Lassiter became Adam's new best friend, as the alien found the Human to be a pressure relief valve for his concerns. And Adam needed an ally. It was obvious he was now a prisoner in the palace, and after a trip beyond his suite, he returned to find his duffle bag missing. He still had the Sig Sauer tucked in his sock, but that weapon only had a ten-shot magazine and no spares. It might be enough to help him acquire more weapons, but that whole scenario was ripe with problems. And his spaceship was fifty miles away—if it was even still there. Wilsom knew where it was hidden.

On the morning of the third day, Alacot came to Adam's room for no other reason than to hide from the increasingly unstable Wilsom.

"I have never seen such a rapid transformation," the alien was saying. "I have known Wilsom for many years, and he is different. I cannot explain it."

Adam smirked. It seemed aliens were just as screwed up as Humans when it came to the trappings of power. Wilsom saw enemies in every shadow, and he'd already summarily executed two of his closest aides for simply questioning his dictates. That put a damper on any further debate. From then on, what Wilsom said was the law.

"Any news on my credits?" Adam asked the advisor.

He shook his head. "All I know is that funds are flowing to maintain the government. That would tell me access has been granted. But there has been no talk of paying you."

"Dammit!" Adam was at his wit's end. He would give it one more day, and then he would have to do something. What that something would be was the sixty-four-thousand-dollar question.

"If you were in charge of Osino, what would you do?" Adam asked Alacot. As far as Adam could tell, Osino was going down fast. At some point, it would reach the breaking point.

"Hypothetically, I would do much. But I am a servant, not a leader."

"You said you study and advise. That's more than your current crop of leaders have done. They seem to simply react."

"That is true. On a planet such as Osino, with such a small population and a single economy, management is required more than leadership. We are a simple society. Allow us to grow the algae and sell it, and everyone will prosper. There is no need for such drama. However, because the algae is such an important commodity, it attracts powerful interests, both here and off-world. These entities seek control rather than cooperation."

"Too bad *you're* not in control."

"It is the last thing I would—"

The door to the suite suddenly burst open, and a team of armed Guards stormed in. Wilsom followed them in.

"So, the conspiracies continue," Wilsom said in a shrill voice. "Are you planning another coup, Human, and with my most *trusted* advisor?" He laughed when he said the word *trusted*. "The Guards have their weapons set at Level-1; yes, Adam, I have studied and learned from you ... and about you. Now, come with me, both of you. There is a reckoning due."

They were taken to Wilsom's office, where two guards flanked the desk with their Xan-fis cradled in their arms. Adam was without his bag of weapons, so Wilsom felt confident that he had the Human under control. But he started off by berating Alacot.

"I have been monitoring your visits to the Human. What is it you seek from him? You know he is a killer. Did you offer him pay to kill me?"

"Of course not, my President. I remain loyal to you. There is no conspiracy afoot."

"Then why all the clandestine meetings? What did you discuss?"

Alacot hesitated. He was trapped between telling

the truth—which could get him killed—or lying to the President—which could also get him killed.

Adam was sitting in a chair on the other side of the expansive desk, watching the guards. Their eyes were on Alacot.

"Speak, Alacot!" Wilsom yelled. "Tell the truth. You have nothing to fear from me."

"I ... I fear that is not so," Alacot muttered.

"When do I get my credits?" Adam asked, trying to deflect the conversation. All it did was send Wilsom into even a higher state of agitation.

"You ask about your credits; the credits you think you are deserving? That is all you are concerned about, while I have a planet to rule! Let me tell you my thinking on the matter. You failed in the first attempt to secure my position. You nearly got me killed, and I had to flee the planet like a scared child. You humiliated me before the population, including my enemies. And now you think you are deserving of a reward for such failure. You will never see any of the credits I—"

Adam reached into his sock and removed the Sig Sauer. Aiming the small handgun at Wilsom, he said, "What the hell." And he pulled the trigger.

The shot was followed by two others in rapid succession, targeting the guards. They were dead before Wilsom's corpse finished recoiling against the back of his chair with his head resting on the back cushion and his mouth hung limp. His eyes were still open.

Adam moved quickly to the guards and took their weapons, hooking the straps around his shoulder. He held the Sig firmly in his grip as he turned to a stunned Alacot Lassiter.

"It looks like you're in charge now."

"Me!" he stammered. "I had nothing to do with this."

"Unfortunately, my little friend here makes a lot of noise, so that's not going to matter in about three seconds. Listen, Alacot, the people know you; they respect you. You have been a force in the government for years. This is your chance to make a difference. You can do this. You just have to step up and take control."

"The desire for control is what has caused this mess."

"You know what I mean. Get ready; the guards are going to be in here any second."

The door burst open, and the guards rushed in.

"Hold!" Alacot said in a commanding voice, much to Adam's surprise. Equally to his surprise, the guards obeyed.

"There has been a reckoning," Alacot began. "I am now assuming control of the government. All of you know Wilsom Panasin, so you know how unstable he has been recently. Today, that instability reached a breaking point, and he took his own life, but not before killing his guards."

Adam shook his head, not believing what he was hearing. But what was even more shocking was the reaction from the soldiers. They surveyed the scene and looked at one another, nodding.

"That seems reasonable," said the lead sergeant. "Is that not so?" he asked the others. They all nodded.

"President Panasin is dead ... and we accept the ascension of Alacot Lassidor to the office." He turned again to the others. "Go and spread the word." He looked at Alacot with exhaustion in his eyes. "Let us hope this is the last transition we will experience for a while, my President."

Adam was dumbfounded by the sudden turn of events. When he pulled his weapon and fired, he truly thought he'd go out in a hail of flash bolts, dying on this godforsaken shithole of a planet. Now he faded into the background as the room flooded with others, both military and civilian. After a brief moment of shock, everyone seemed relieved at Wilsom's death and rushed to congratulate the new President on his promotion. It was as quick and seamless as that.

But then Alacot pulled Adam aside.

"There is a transport waiting for you outside. Please make haste and leave Osino as quickly as possible. There may be loyalists of Wilsom who will not accept the official version of events. I know I would not."

"Yeah, that was pretty slick ... and unexpected. Now, about my credits."

Alacot frowned. "Are you serious? Everyone here knows what truly happened. If I paid you credits from the treasury, it would look as though *I* hired you to kill President Panasin. Consider yourself fortunate that you are leaving with your life. I am sure Wilsom had no intention of ever letting you walk out of here alive. But now, I do want to thank you for your effective and very impulsive act, but now it is time for you and Osino to part ways."

"And without my money?"

"Unfortunately, it was never *your* money—your credits. And neither was it Wilsom's to give. Those credits belong to the citizens of Osino. Consider it a gift you give to the people. It will be much appreciated."

---

As Adam climbed into the driver's seat of the transport and set out on the road to Shallows, all he kept saying to himself over and over again was, "Tidus is going to kill me!"

## 11

The journey back to Tel'oran was telling. It only took eight days, but during that time, Tidus made no attempt to reach Adam. Nor did Adam call him. The transponder on the ship was active, so Tidus knew he was in transit.

In this case, Adam's philosophy was, 'Put off until tomorrow what you will get your ass chewed out for today.' Nevertheless, they would have to face each other eventually.

'Eventually' was three hours after the CX-91 touched down at the executive spaceport outside the Tel'oran capital city of Dal Innis. Adam offloaded his gear to his ship, the *Arieel*, before taking his car into town. He had no idea if he'd have a job after this. That worried him since, technically, the *Arieel* belonged to Starfire Security. If anything, Adam deserved the ship as part of a severance package. That got him thinking: He didn't have a severance package negotiated with Tidus. Perhaps this was the time to put one together ... just in case.

Adam timed the arrival on the planet to coincide with early morning. Tidus usually took a few hours to wake up fully, and if Adam could catch him when he was half awake, the browbeating might not be as severe. Unfortunately, when Adam entered the former Juirean Overlord's office, it was obvious he'd been up all night, unable to sleep, tormented by the things he had to say to Adam.

This time, there were no congratulations and no offer of a Diet Pepsi after a successful mission. In a way, Osino *was* a victory. The old President had been replaced, just not with the person expected, although that did happen ... for about a day. Missions seldom proceeded as planned. It was more about the final result than anything else. At least that's what Adam kept telling himself.

Tidus was right at seven feet tall and with the customary angular face and radically pointed chin as most Juireans. His flamboyant bouffant-style mane of blue Overlord hair had been replaced decades ago with a now-grey, butt-length ponytail that made Tidus look like an aging Hippie from Earth. However, the green skin and golden eyes betrayed his appearance as an alien. And this particular alien was fighting mightily to maintain his composure. Adam wished he'd stop all the pretense and just get it over with. Tidus wasn't doing a very good job of hiding his emotions.

His normally thin lips were but hairlines on his face, and the slender neck pulsated with matching veins on each side dancing in unison. It was hypnotic, distracting Adam for a moment from what was to come.

"What do you have to say for yourself?" Tidus began using the cliché mothers used when confronting their unruly children with the truth of their actions.

"In the end, Osino is going to be better off." It wasn't much of an excuse, but it was what spurted from his mouth. In the heat of the moment, Adam suddenly forgot all the smooth and convincing arguments he had spent days rehearsing.

"Yes, I have heard. The news has filtered out that one of our clients—once achieving his goal of the Presidency, suddenly decided to end his life. How convenient. Although the details are sketchy, few believe the story. Yet, this is Osino, so nobody really cares. To reference your homeworld, Osino is like a third-world country with a single valuable export crop. As long as the algae ships, everyone is happy."

"The spice must flow," Adam muttered under his breath.

Tidus didn't catch what he said, which only irritated him more. "Speak up, dammit! You sit there like a petulant child. Your very demeanor tells me you know how badly you screwed up! Adam, we are not assassins. If Starfire developed that reputation, we might as well close our doors. In all the years I worked for Priority Acquisitions, we never overtly engaged in contract kills."

"Not overtly, but many of your mercenary operations did just that."

"It's different when there's a war being waged, and we're hired to represent one side or the other."

"We were."

"And that operation failed!" Tidus screamed. "That should have been the end of it. We were paid, and all accounts were settled."

"But they weren't," Adam countered.

"You mean Dracu Hor? Of course, the bastard betrayed you—betrayed us. And there would have probably been a reckoning at some point. But that would have been Starfire settling a score. Instead, you take a paying job to assassinate a sitting planetary head-of-state."

"Along with Dracu."

"Do not play games with me."

"I took the assignment on my own. It was not a Starfire sanctioned operation."

"Do you think anyone will believe that? This isn't about what was and what wasn't. This is about perception. You are *The Human*, probably the most high-profile recovery agent and mercenary in the galaxy. Your identity is inexorably tied to Starfire in everything you do. It is part of our branding. Too many people on Osino know who you are, and the fact that you were present at the time of the assassinations, they will draw their own conclusions. And in this case, they will be right. And then that little stunt of dressing Dracu up like a Human. Clever but transparent. Sure, you didn't kill him. But you *had* him killed. It's the same thing."

"It seemed like a good idea at the time."

Tidus stared hard at Adam for a moment before blowing out a gust of air from his mouth. "There you go again. You take nothing seriously. I am trying to run a legitimate business here, and now I have an agent who goes rogue and runs his own operation in plain sight of everyone. This will come back on my company and me."

Adam felt like shit and about three feet tall. "I'm sorry, Tidus. I didn't mean to make it hard on you or Starfire. I let my anger get the best of me."

"Anger? Bullshit! I talked with Indo. I know about the million-and-a-half energy credits. I know you were *officially* off the books," he put *officially* in finger quotes, "but I think a fair amount of those credits should go to Starfire to help repair some of the damage our reputation has suffered. It's only fair."

Adam's face must have turned beet red because Tidus noticed. "What is wrong with you? You look as if you just swallowed a bug. To a Juirean, that is not a bad thing. But to a Human, I know that is bad."

When Adam remained silent, Tidus began to suspect something was wrong. "What is it? What are you not telling me?"

Adam took a deep breath. "Well, there's no easy way to say this, but I was stiffed on the credits."

"You mean you don't have any in Human-speak?"

"That's right. They reneged on our agreement."

Tidus stared at Adam with disbelief. "Perhaps shooting the client through the eye might have been the reason you weren't paid."

"It was just above the eye ... and besides, it was obvious he had no intention of paying me. That's one of the reasons I shot him."

"And the other?"

"He was an asshole."

Tidus pushed back from his desk and bellowed out a laugh. "Then, by all means, assassinate the asshole. In Adam Cain's World, that is a capital offense. In that case, I'm surprised *I'm* still alive."

"So am I," Adam said with an embarrassed smile. This was perhaps the wrong time for levity.

The grin evaporated from the Juirean's face. "Give me one good reason why I should not fire your ass on the spot. Please, make your argument."

"I'm the best bounty hunter you have," Adam said quickly. "And I have other talents, as you know."

"Like assassinations?"

"That, and other things. C'mon, Tidus, you know you're not going to fire me. This was a minor thing."

"Losing a million-and-a-half credit is a minor thing to you?"

"Yeah, that was pretty bad. But, you know, live and learn."

"Dammit, Adam, you've lived longer than most, and if you don't get yourself prematurely killed, you're going to outlive us all. I would expect more from you. You may look young, but you're not. You have too much experience to let something like this happen. I was going to let you slide for a fair amount of your fee. But you've come back empty-handed. Again I ask, what am I to do with you?"

"Let me make it up to you," Adam said quickly, seeing his opening.

"How?"

"Let me do what I do best, go grab a high-bounty fugitive. And no bonus this time."

"Bonus? Why the hell should I pay you anything? You owe me."

Adam recoiled. He wasn't expecting that.

"That's not really fair, now is it?"

"Fair is me keeping you on the payroll. Anything beyond that is the bonus."

There was an awkward moment of silence as the

two friends locked eyes with one another. Tidus broke the staring contest first.

"Fine, but make it a good one. And instead of your standard forty percent, only thirty. And no bonus!"

"Perfect. I'll do it," Adam agreed.

"But make it a good one. I was expecting quite a few credits from your Osino escapade. I know it won't make up for it, but it will be a start. Use the computer in the outer office and check the Boards. I want a definite target and a plan before you leave here today."

Adam popped up out of the chair and headed for the door. "No problem, Boss. I'll find the largest bounty out there."

"One every swinging dick in the galaxy will be going after? I would like more of a sure thing."

Adam stopped at the door and turned. "Hey, you're talking to *The Human*. Everything I do is a sure thing."

Adam's silly grin vanished immediately as he heard the words he spoke. He was through the doorway before the clock that had once been on Tidus's desk flew into the wall next to the door, shattering on impact. Adam was fortunate aliens had terrible aim.

## 12

The Boards Tidus spoke of were the galactic registry of open warrants. It was maintained by the Formilians and disseminated through the same process that brought the Galactic Library to every corner of the Milky Way.

Adam was interested in the new warrants, the ones that hadn't had time to be worked. Many of the older ones were called dead warrants since the perpetrator was more than likely dead. Criminals lived dangerous lives and ran in dangerous circles. Either that or the warrant had been filled, and neither the recovery company nor the issuing party saw fit to clear the document from the Boards. That meant you could spend days, weeks and even months searching for someone who had already faced justice, one way or another. The new ones were ripe and ready for picking.

He set the lower limit at seventy-five thousand credits and searched the standard limits. The default setting was to start low and work your way up, so it was purely by luck that Adam spotted a warrant that caught his attention.

It was for the apprehension and return of an individual wanted for multiple homicides, the theft of a starship and the kidnapping of a prominent citizen. What caught his attention was the issuing planet. It was Anarea, and the person sought in the warrant was known only as *The Human*.

Adam chuckled. He knew this was for one of his most recent operations and involved the capture of Jorvis Canara, a major crime lord on the planet. During the mission, a few lives were lost, and Adam's starship was stolen, requiring his appropriation of another vessel to go after the thieves. The seventy-five-thousand-credit-bounty undoubtedly came from the crime boss's escrowed funds since he was rotting away somewhere in a Zanorian prison.

This wasn't the first time Adam had seen a warrant for his arrest; in fact, he checked every few weeks to see if anything new showed up. It was common for Indie security personnel such as him to run into this kind of trouble. When one thought about it, nearly every apprehension on an alien world was breaking the local law, either for kidnapping, false imprisonment or a host of other creative crimes. It was hard to avoid. As he often thought, one person's villain was another person's saint, and with the individuality of planets and their laws, there was very little respect for the laws of others. A killer on one world was an innocent on another. Capturing him to take him back to the proper jurisdiction was an iffy proposition. Most of the top-rated worlds respected the laws of others and turned a blind eye to the practice. But on less developed worlds, often run by the criminals or beholden to their payola, they got downright militant about so-called abuses taking place within their jurisdiction.

Adam didn't worry much about the warrant. It was an unspoken agreement among bounty hunters that they didn't hunt their kind. If they did, then the next week, it might be them in shackles and heading back to some obscure world on which they'd spent a few days doing a recovery operation.

Still, Adam thought it funny and a little insulting. Only seventy-five thousand. Hell, he killed a precinct worth of dirty cops and the gangster's capo. He shrugged. He did feel bad about hijacking the mule-ship, but he was desperate. Hopefully, the ship was returned to the owners.

But now, he got down to business. He scanned forward to the higher bounties. They usually capped out at around four hundred thousand. After that, the quest for justice became counterproductive. It didn't make sense to pay more than the crime was worth just to bring someone to court. Four hundred thousand would go a long way to smoothing Tidus's feathers if he had feathers. He didn't. And thirty percent to Adam was a nice little sum of one-hundred-twenty kay, even without a bonus.

The problem with the higher bounties, as Tidus had alluded to, was all the big recovery companies would be after it. Some would even have teams assigned, seeing that the payoff was worth it. It also attracted a lot of rookies who saw it as a way of making a quick score and then moving on. But these bigger bounties, discounting the crowded competition, often meant bigger crooks with more security. It often took a team to catch them. But Adam wasn't interested in that. If so, then he'd have to split his thirty percent with the other team members while Tidus still kept seventy percent for the company. No, he would do it himself.

Then out of curiosity, Adam scrolled even more to the high-limit bounties. These were usually reserved for political figures, like ex-presidents who absconded with the treasury, such as Esson Creel was about to do, at least to a degree. These types of operations required teams and months, if not years, of tracking, planning and execution. Adam wasn't interested in that either. He wanted something he could do in a hurry.

And then he saw something that caught his eye. It was in the higher range, paying a million-credit bounty. He read the data sheet.

It seemed that a creature name Nija Falonmore stole twenty-five million credits from the company she worked for and fled the planet. It happened only sixteen days before, and this was the first day the warrant was on the Boards. This wasn't a political figure, just an opportunist who pressed a few buttons on a computer and was suddenly fabulously wealthy. Good for her.

He dug deeper. She had no past criminal affiliations, so she would have no large organization protecting her. And no priors, either. Just as he thought: an opportunist.

Next the location. She was from the planet Kalicor, which according to the attached map, was only seventy light-years from Tel'oran: a three-day journey in the *Arieel*. That was if she had gone home after the theft. Checking further, he saw that the issuing warrant was from the planet Tactori. He'd been there before. It was a high-tech world with a lot of big finance companies. She must have worked for one of them. This also meant that all or part of the bounty was coming from the company. They had to set an example to keep others from stealing from them, hence the million-credit bounty.

He checked the boxes: Rookie perpetrator; not too

well-traveled or connected; an amount of credits that would be hard to hide; and located almost next door to Tel'oran. It would also be the largest bounty he'd ever gone after.

Even so, something like this would attract a lot of attention. He had to hurry.

Adam copied the file to his datapad and then rushed back to Tidus's office.

"I got something you might like," Adam said quickly as he entered without knocking. He didn't want to give Tidus time to locate another object to throw at him. "It pays a million."

Tidus leaned back in his chair and stretched out a sad smile. It wasn't the expression Adam was expecting.

"Sit down, Adam; let me tell you about million-credit-bounties."

Cautiously, he took a chair. He sensed Tidus was still mad at him.

"What about them, except it's a lot of money."

"And there's the problem. How much did they steal, ten, twenty million, maybe twenty-five?"

'Twenty-five; how did you know?'"

"Just think about it," Tidus began. "Oh, wait, thinking is something you don't do too good. I'll explain. I'll talk slowly so you'll understand."

Adam smirked. Tidus smirked back.

"Do you really think people who just had twenty-five million credits stolen from them are really after justice, to find the perpetrator and then lock them up for twenty years or more? Hell, no. What they want is their money back or at least part of it. That's what the million-credit bounty says."

"Okay, but how do they get their money back?"

"Think, Adam. Think. If you had twenty-five million credits and someone came to arrest you, what would you do?"

"I'd hire the best security to keep me safe."

Tidus shook his head. "No, you wouldn't."

"I wouldn't?"

"No, you would instead bribe the bounty hunter with some of your ill-gotten gains, and usually a fair amount. That's how these high-limit bounties go."

"You sound like you're okay with that. I thought we weren't supposed to take bribes. That's against the rules. You got mad at me for doing a couple of justified assassinations. What would it do to our reputation if we let fugitives go in exchange for a few credits?"

"As I said, that's how these things go. But it's a little more complicated. Usually, the bribe money is given back to the people who had it stolen from them in the first place. They don't pay the bounty because you didn't bring in the fugitive, but they usually will let you keep ten to twenty percent of the amount recovered."

Adam sat back in the chair, his mind working.

"How much is the bribe money on twenty-five million, usually."

"I'd be expecting ten million, simply from the amount of the original bounty. Ten percent would be a million, twenty, two million. Besides the payoff to the recovery company, there are other reasons a bribe is preferred over an apprehension. One, the warrant gets lifted, and two, the company gets at least some of its money back. Putting someone in jail and throwing away the key seldom results in recovery of the funds, not even part of it."

Adam was beginning to see why something like this was different than a standard recovery. "It sounds almost as if the crook will be expecting this to happen. They steal the money and then give part of it back to lift the warrant. The company gets some of their money back, and the recovery company is paid out of that money, and not anything new they have to fork over."

Tidus's eyes lit up. "I believe young Mr. Cain just passed the final exam. Good for him. But first, do you see the problem this can pose?"

Adam's mind raced. He couldn't see a downside. They had a chance to make as much as double the bounty, and they didn't even have to bring anyone in. He slowly shook his head.

"It's what I said before. Every bounty hunter in the region will be after this score. And the fugitive, if they know anything about how this works, will already have a portion of their credits set aside. They'll be anxious to do a deal just so they can get the warrant lifted. But that also means they need to do business with someone they can trust to turn the bribe money over and to get the warrant lifted."

Adam sat up in the chair, excited now after the lesson Tidus had just delivered. "You said it earlier; I'm one of the most famous bounty hunters in the galaxy. The female who took these credits may even feel honored to have me represent her."

"You're also known for bringing in your man, or alien, or alien female. You know what I mean. You're beyond reproach, at least when it comes to bounty hunting."

"Hey, I can be just as unscrupulous as the next guy. I can take a bribe. Just watch me."

"That's funny," Tidus said. "You're bragging about taking a bribe. I think you are ready for the big show."

"Then I have your sanction?"

Tidus nodded. "Just be careful. There will be some who only see the bounty money. Others will think this is their domain, and you'll be intruding. For experienced operators, they know the bounty money is just the base. They know how to play the game better than you."

"Yeah, well, you wait and see. I'm a fast learner."

Tidus looked at his desk, seemingly confused. Then

he pursed his thin lips and looked across the room at his shattered clock. "I was going to say you better hurry. This bounty just went up today, and I'll bet there's already a parade of starships headed for Kalicor. And that's assuming that's where she is. It's going to get crowded, Adam. Be forewarned."

## 13

Adam rushed back to the *Arieel* and prepared for lift-off. He checked the fuel pods, the chemical propellant and the food stocks. He'd been away for three months and couldn't remember if everything was charged up. When he left for the office that morning, he had no idea he'd be heading back out so soon.

He lifted and set a course for Kalicor. He'd never been there before; in fact, he'd never heard of the planet, and it was only seventy light-years from Tel'oran. That wasn't unusual. There were millions of planets in the galaxy, including tens of thousands of what were considered Prime worlds, those capable of supporting Juirean life. It wasn't considered Humanoid life because the Juireans were the ones who set the benchmarks, such as they did with Juirean standard gravity. That was about three-quarters of Earth's. Adam often wondered why the vast majority of worlds in the former Expansion—and later in the Human's Orion-Cygnus Union—had lower gravity than Earth. But that was the case, with .75 being the standard. Although a weird coincidence, Adam welcomed it still the same. It was what set Humans apart from the rest of the aliens in the galaxy, allowing them to excel with regard to strength and quickness. Not only that, but the heavy gravity of Earth helped durable and robust creatures evolve, creatures that would one day dominate the galaxy in multiple categories. Adam often referred to himself as being superhuman, but that was wrong. He was *superalien*. On Earth, he was just a Human with nothing super about it. But when compared to aliens, he was badass.

The Formilian's Galactic Library was always the first place to go when doing a trace. Although Adam had never made an entry into the galactic internet, somehow information got uploaded, and often some of the most obscure facts. With countless trillions upon trillions of Primes on the civilized planets, he was often amazed at how even normal people ended up with a profile. He didn't know if that was good or bad, preferring more privacy than most. But he was a public figure and had been for decades. He used to check his profile in the Library, surprised at the information that could be had. Of course, a lot of it was myth or outright lies. But on average, it was fairly accurate, fact-based-mythology, he called it. And yet, there were so many events in his life that weren't in the library. And thank god they weren't.

And that was why he preferred to be called simply *The Human*. He couldn't hide his race, but he could hide his identity, at least for a while.

The Library is where he began his search for Nija Falonmore. He wasn't surprised when he found a listing, in fact, nineteen thousand of them, and from a variety of planets. It seemed it was a very popular name among aliens.

Narrowing the search to just Kalicor dropped the number to forty-eight hundred, and then searching for those who worked in the financial industry narrowed it even more, down to seventy-one. Adam had no idea as to her age or her appearance, but he had a way to find out.

He checked news reports from Tactori regarding any recent thefts of large sums of money. The planet was a financial hub, and as such, they took great pride in the security of the system. There was a chance they would keep such a theft secret, especially since it was an inside job. Fortunately, there was an entry, along with an attached police report, that required a special access code to open. Adam had one such code, thanks to Tidus and his years at Priority Acquisitions.

As the largest security and fugitive recovery

company in the galaxy, PA had all kinds of special equipment and codes they provided their agents, and over the years, Tidus accumulated quite the treasure trove of goodies that set his new company apart from most of the others. Priority operated at a time when the Expansion was still intact, so interstellar crime was frowned upon. Planets cooperated with each other to make it as hard on criminals as possible, and PA was their go-to asset. That all changed with the Klin invasion and the disintegration of the Expansion. Now, very few planets cooperated. It was a chaotic time but also one ripe with opportunity for people like Adam and Tidus.

Adam laughed, thinking how easy it was for him to find information. It was almost too easy. But then he cringed. If he could find this much information while traveling through interstellar space, then so could others. There was no shortage of recovery agents operating in the galaxy these days.

But now he had a picture of the culprit. As he suspected, she was fairly young, around twenty-eight in Kalicor years. He had no idea as to the life expectancy of the species, so it could have been either young or old. It didn't matter. He had her picture. The Kalicoreans were almost scarily like Humans, with only a few noticeable exceptions. They had pointed ears, like elves, and flabbier jowls—well, flabbier than some Humans. They were also taller, with the average alien being six and a half feet tall. Nija Falonmore had flaming red hair and a pale complexion. For an alien, she was cute. Really cute.

The confidential police report verified the amount stolen and that the credits had been transferred into another account over a period of twenty-four days, with hard chips then being withdrawn over that time. That meant Nija absconded with what was essentially cash and not just a data file. Twenty-five million in energy credit chips would be quite the load. He wondered how she got them off the planet…?

The theft took place over two months but was discovered eleven days after Nija drained her second account. Eight days after that, the warrant was issued, appearing that morning on the Boards. By then, Nija was long gone.

Her last day on the job had been twenty-two days ago. Adam figured she left the planet immediately and with a fairly large crate of energy credits that would require a special shipping ticket. She could afford it, especially if she paid cash. That also meant she had the assets to hire a private starship to get off Tactori, one which would be hard to trace. But Adam had a way around that, too.

After going through the requisite check of the public passenger manifests for flights leaving around twenty-two days ago—and finding no name matches—he used another access code to check private spaceliners heading out from Tactori. The number was huge, so he reversed the search, focusing on liners coming to Kalicor from Tactori. After factoring in the average travel time from planet to planet, he ended up with nine ships.

That didn't seem like too many to track, but they landed all over the planet. It's like saying nine airplanes landed in nine airports on Earth. That didn't narrow the search down too much. And this was assuming Nija returned to her homeworld. But he had to start somewhere, and in a galaxy of alien worlds, first instinct was to always head for one's homeworld. And to one's hometown.

But Adam had seventy-one name possibilities, again assuming she was traveling under her real name. If Adam had just stolen twenty-five mill, he would be using an alias. But she might be traveling using her real face.

He had the computer check the image he had of her—a corporate ID photo—with any on file for the seventy-one possibilities. No luck. But Adam did have another piece of specialized equipment provided to all the agents from Starfire Security. He had the computer match birth photos against the one he had of the older Nija Falonmore using a method of de-aging that converted a photo back to the time of birth. It wasn't perfect, but it did narrow his search down to three possibilities. That was better. Checking the hometowns with the nearest spaceports gave him a place to start. Two of the names had hometowns near where the private liners landed. He now looked for more modern files on the two suspects, including current and former addresses, relatives, friends, and other official documents, including professional licenses. It was scary how many files there were on—well, everyone—and all on the galactic internet.

Only a couple of hours into his three-day trip to Kalicor, he knew where Nija Falonmore was born, where she was raised, where she received her training in finance and her entire work history. He had her friends, relatives and even mates listed. He also had the arrival times of two ships from Tactori around the time she would have been arriving.

The only thing he wasn't sure of was her current location. She'd been working for Bandors Bank for only a month when she began withdrawing the funds. That meant at least three to four months of living on Tactori. That wasn't too long. Did she also maintain a home on Kalicor? He had two addresses to check out in two different cities thousands of miles apart. But again, it was better than what he started with, which was nothing. And again, this was all assuming she came home after the theft.

Adam fixed dinner, satisfied with the work he'd done so far. It troubled him, however, that most of the information he'd accessed was in the public domain.

But it bothered him more knowing that with the right pedigree—or enough money to buy what you needed—a whole other level of data was accessible.

With Tidus's stolen access codes, Adam had access to the flight logs of the various spaceports; he could find shipping manifests, as well as confidential police files from thousands of worlds. He had backdoor access to banking records, shopping habits and even weapon purchases, plus a whole lot more. This made the tracking of fugitives fairly easy, up to a point. However, eventually, it came down to boots on the ground and knocking on doors.

And Starfire wasn't the only company with backdoor codes. All the serious companies had them. And that was why Adam had to assume other bounty hunters knew as much as he did, if not more. It would be a race to see who got to Nija Falonmore first.

And Adam had to be on his toes. Recovery agents were an eclectic group of individuals coming from all backgrounds and with a full spectrum of morals. He wouldn't put anything past them, especially with so many credits in play.

## 14

Adam picked the first spaceport out of the two by pure chance. It seemed that the accessible shipping manifests for both spaceliners were lacking in detail. They each brought in passengers and cargo, although there were no descriptions of the clients or the contents of the packages. There wasn't even security camera footage of the departing passengers, something he could use to match the photo he had. Whoever was on both those ships wished to remain anonymous. With luck, one of them was Nija Falonmore.

The planet Kalicor was a seven-rated world technologically, making it reasonably civilized. Compare that to

Earth's *two* rating just before the Juirean attack forty years ago, and you get some idea of what the planet was like. And the more technologically advanced a world was, the easier it was to track someone.

However, Nija had absconded with a small fortune. She would be aware she was being hunted, so she wouldn't make it easy on the hunter.

Adam landed at a spaceport with the largest nearby city being Qinloc. One of Adam's Nija Falonmores was from there, showing a current address and a registered mate.

Adam went through the normal after-landing procedures observed by most civilized planets, even having to declare his carried MK-17 flash weapon. His Starfire Security ID allowed him to keep it. He kept the weapon in a shoulder holster he wore under his waist-length jacket. He didn't have any hybrid weapons with him simply because he hadn't had time to build another one after losing the two he had on Osino.

Entering the concourse, he made for the transport rental section. He walked at a quick pace and then would suddenly stop and go in the opposite direction for a few steps, trying to catch anyone who was following him. Already, he had three prospects and one definite.

*Damn, they got here quickly.*

It was obvious they knew who he was and were

going to piggyback on his investigation. That meant a confrontation at some time in the near future.

Adam rented a transport and then raced to get to it, hoping to catch the bounty hunters following him off guard. He had his datapad set with Nija's last known location—at least this Nija Falonmore.

The streets and buildings of the alien city were both familiar and comforting, reminding him of Earth. It was the same with most advanced Prime worlds. Since all Primes were of the same basic form and breathed very near the same mixture of atmosphere, their wants, needs and desires often coincided with those of other Primes. That meant buildings were mainly above ground and box-shaped. Transports—cars—ran on four wheels since there was no such thing as anti-gravity. Even the clothing was similar since it had to cover the same basic body form. Add to that the need for food and shelter, meaningful labor and for procreation of the species, and most alien worlds *The Human* visited didn't seem that alien at all. And, of course, the Kalicoreans were more familiar-looking than most. They were an attractive species. Their pointed ears were cute, as he said in an elf-like way, and not like a Vulcan's.

Adam kept checking the rearview camera for signs of a tail. Again, there were possibilities. But the deeper he got into the neighborhood, the less he began to believe this was the Nija Falonmore he was looking for. It was a decidedly rundown community with stacked boxes making up the housing. Some climbed five cubes high since the lot sizes were tiny. The computer led him to an address with only two small boxes attached to one another, tiny even for this neighborhood.

Adam noticed the other transport pull to the side down the street when he stopped in front of the house.

He jumped out and unabashedly strode to the front door. This was a waste of time, but he had to check it off his list. He rapped on the metal door.

An irritated male native answered. Adam could read the emotion on the alien face as the tall creature leaned in closer to him as if he were about to attack. Adam wasn't worried.

"I told the others she is not the one you seek. Leave us alone before I call the authorities. What is this all about that you suddenly descend on our home?"

"It's just a misunderstanding," Adam said. "Sorry to bother you."

If anything, this raised the prospect of the *next* Nija being the right one. And if someone had already been here, then that meant they were a step ahead.

He sprinted back to the car, got in and then spun around in the street, heading back the way he came. He stopped next to the transport that had been following him.

He waved his fingers across his throat. "This isn't

the one; don't bother. He may call the cops on you if you knock on his door again."

The two creatures, each of different alien races, at first tried to ignore him and hide their faces. Then they turned and nodded sheepishly.

Adam had to hurry back to the spaceport. He needed to make a quick hop to the next location before he lost the light ... and before he lost the bounty.

---

Adam entered the spaceport in a rush, not caring who was following him. Even so, he spotted a familiar face. It wasn't a friend, but a rare acquaintance, and not someone you easily forgot.

Mada Niac nodded at Adam from his table, where he sat with three others, each with the look of seasoned bounty hunters. The fact that Mada was sitting nonchalantly in a restaurant at the spaceport—rather than racing off to the city of Ualic—spoke volumes.

Still, Adam had to hurry.

He reached his ship a few minutes later, and when he entered, he immediately sensed something wasn't right.

The metal bar came down on his head and sent him to the deck. He could tolerate pain better than most, so the fact that the blow didn't kill him came as a surprise to his assailant. It was a surprise to Adam, as well. The hit was supposed to have split open his skull.

He lay on the deck, still breathing and barely conscious. He would heal faster, but that was if he were given a chance. He didn't think he would.

Through blurry eyes, Adam could see four aliens rummaging through his ship. He wasn't sure if they'd been in there when he arrived or if they followed him through the airlock. If anything, he needed to get a new lock for the door. People breaking into his ship was becoming a habit.

They were at his computer and his files, stuffing all they could find into a canvas pouch. These were other bounty hunters, probably the ones who followed him to the house. They were too lazy to do their own research, so they would just steal it from a more accomplished and skilled operative.

In his condition, he was vulnerable. Once the thieves were done rifling through his ship and discovered he was still alive, they would undoubtedly finish the job. *The Human* had a reputation for holding grudges. As long as he lived, he'd be a threat.

## 15

Suddenly there was a disturbance at the airlock, the sound of flash bolts and the thumping of flesh. There was a mad scramble in the common room as the four invaders fought against another group of huge aliens. Damn, it was crowded in Adam's tiny ship, with people stepping on and tripping over his inert body. He moaned when a creature tumbled over him before making a mad dash out of the airlock.

Calm returned to the ship, but Adam wasn't alone. Hands were helping him up, and a wet compress was applied to his bleeding scalp. He was placed on a couch and propped up with pillows. He felt better, and his eyesight was returning.

He found himself staring into the black eyes of Mada Niac. One of the other bounty hunters held the compress against the back of Adam's head while the other two set about straightening the compartment. The canvas bag with his computer and datapads was resting on a table, having been recovered from the thieves.

"I guess I should say thanks," Adam groaned, his focus returning but with the room still spinning.

"It was a professional courtesy," a huge alien said.

"How have you been, Mada; it's been a while."

"Indeed it has. I know your reputation; even so, I hope you hold no grudges for the incident on Ennock Bin. It was only business."

"I hear that a lot. But considering what you just did for me, I'd say we're even."

Mada shook his head. "Lazy and unprofessional," he said, referring to the thieves. "We saw them follow you through the concourse. There were only two, so the others must have already been on your ship."

Adam tried to stand, but he didn't get far before falling back onto the couch. "Give me a minute, and I'll be fine. Thanks again, but now, I don't mean to be rude, but you have to leave. I have places to go—"

"To Ualic? Do not bother; she is not there."

Of course, Mada would know about Ualic. And Adam had to believe him; if she were, then Mada and his team wouldn't be here, and fortuitously saving Adam's life.

"It is our conclusion that the name Nija Falonmore

was appropriated as a cover by our fugitive. And since the theft happened so soon after she began working for Bandors Bank, it is our belief that she is a professional and the theft and cover story were planned ahead of time."

Even through the fog of his injury, Adam had to accept what Mada said was true. He and his team were unique in the security business. They specialized in high-limit jobs, hiring themselves out to *other* security companies when the price was right. He had a reputation even greater than Adam's and was based solely on his effectiveness as a hunter. Adam's came mainly from the race he belonged to.

"Then she's in the wind—gone."

"Not necessarily, my friend." Mada waved to one of his team, and Adam was brought a drink from the food processor. He took the glass and chugged it. It made him feel better. "Easy with that," Mada said. "It may affect your injured brain."

Adam smirked. He would heal much faster than a normal Human and magnitudes faster than an alien. Thanks to Mada's timely intervention, he would get the chance. Adam would be back to a hundred percent in only a couple of hours.

Mada continued talking; why Adam didn't know. He was revealing data that was best held close to the vest for people in their line of work.

"As a professional, our target must know how this

works. She would be constantly hunted unless she can negotiate a lifting of the warrant."

"Then why make herself hard to find?" Adam asked. "Why use a cutout, a fake name?"

Mada shrugged his broad shoulders. Most aliens were larger than Humans, and Mada was the rule and not the exception. Towering over eight feet tall, he was also a hulk of a creature, exceptionally toned and in excellent condition. His team mirrored their leader, although they were of different races. He'd personally recruited them over the years, and now they were the top team in the fugitive recovery business.

"Perhaps it is a test. She knows the bounty would attract multitudes of hunters. Some will be only after the million credits, not knowing how to negotiate for the warrant release. Others will be inexperienced and could foul the negotiations, leaving her to give up more of her gains than is necessary. There could be multiple reasons why she is staying hidden. But if she is indeed a professional, she may have set parameters for the team—or individual—she is willing to work with. And for the potential recovery fee, she should get the best." Mada smiled, showing a brilliant set of rounded white teeth, knowing that the Human would not take the gesture as a death challenge.

"Even so, she could be anywhere."

Mada shook his head. "No, she *is* here, and she is watching. I sense it. And now, there is much to discuss,

Adam Cain. Yes, I know who you are, and I have studied your history. Impressive … and confusing. I am aware of Humans, yet not that you age so slowly. You certainly do not look your chronological age."

Adam frowned an expression that stretched the skin and made his head spasm in pain. The other bounty hunter handed Adam a clean, moist compress. The other one was soaked with blood. "What do you think we have to discuss? You're obviously several steps ahead of me in searching for the fugitive. And you can't sweet talk me out of my research, not like the others tried brute force to get."

"I do not need your research. What I seek, however, is a partnership."

"What are you talking about?"

"Accept the truth, Adam Cain; my team and I are more experienced in this type of hunt. However, you are also skilled. As we continue to track down the elusive Nija Falonmore—or whatever her true name is—we will continue to trip over each other. And besides, I may be well-known within our industry, but as a Human, you have a reputation that goes beyond simply bounty hunting. If what I believe is true, then teaming up may prompt our bounty to come to *us*. She will not be able to rest until the warrant removal is negotiated. I feel we have considerable wealth simply waiting for us both if we present ourselves as a unified front."

"That's a lot of assumptions."

"Indeed. Can you fault them?"

Adam shrugged, and his head spasmed again. What he really wanted was for his uninvited guests to leave so he could wallow in pain in private.

"Even if all you say is true, I don't have the authority to team up with you."

"Of course, you don't. Please check with my good friend and former PA associate, Tidus. Tell him I offer to split what recovery fee we receive in half. And consider, not to be insulting, but I have more experience negotiating higher commissions than you. I will be able to get more credits for all of us. Please, link with Tidus. I have his private number if you have forgotten it."

Adam smirked. No, he hadn't forgotten the number; Mada was just showing off. Years ago, Tidus and he worked for the same company; now, they were quasi-competitors. But Adam had to admit it would be better working *with* Mada and his team than working against them. And who knows, with his superior negotiating skills, Adam and Tidus may still come out making just as much as they would have if Adam continued on his own. Besides, Adam felt he owed the bounty hunter. He'd just saved his life. That more than trumped what happened on Ennock Bin two years ago. That was simply a sleight of hand trick that cost Adam his bounty. Chalk it up to Mada's superior skills at the time and Adam's naivety.

Adam nodded slightly so his head wouldn't hurt.

"Okay, I'll check with Tidus."

"Good!" Mada said, standing. His people were already headed for the airlock door. "Then it is as good as settled. We will meet again in the morning. I have some ideas as to how we can flush out the cunning Nija Falonmore. As I said, she is probably watching at this very moment. It will not be long now."

---

"Can you trust him?" Tidus asked over the link.

"Can *I* trust him? Can *you*? You know him better than I do. All I did was butt heads against him a couple of times. You used to work with him."

"We never actually did any missions together. We were both at about the same level of reputation within PA. It was more competitive than congenial."

"That doesn't answer the question. Do I team up with him or not?"

"And *now* he asks for my permission."

"C'mon, Tidus! Dammit, my head hurts. Make a decision, so I can get some rest."

"Sure, go ahead, work with him. As he said, he'll probably get more of a recovery fee than you could anyway, no offense intended. It could benefit us in the long run. But be careful. He is now an independent, and that makes him loyal only to himself."

"Okay, fine. I'll keep that in mind. But now, hang up. I need some sleep."

"You know you are not supposed to sleep after a head injury. You could die in your slumber."

"This time, I would welcome it."

Tidus laughed. "Take care of yourself. And get back here as soon as you can. We desperately need the cash flow."

## 16

The next morning, Adam met Mada and his team at the restaurant in the spaceport concourse.

"You appear miraculously healed," Mada commented. "I can hardly see a bump."

Adam felt the back of his head. Yes, the wound was almost totally healed. He'd noticed that when he suffered more serious injuries, the cloning process that was slowly regrowing his body seemed to accelerate. Not only did the wounds heal faster, but he felt more invigorated and clear of mind as if the chemical process was stimulating his entire body. After the initial pain subsided, the sensation was like being on a strong narcotic. Then once the wound was healed, he returned to a more mellow, constant state of being. He knew that eventually, the cloning would end, and he would regret losing this sense of euphoria that came from the healing process. Of course, he had to suffer a catastrophic injury for the feeling to truly kick in. That was a drawback.

He surveyed the table of hulking alien bounty hunters. Mada was the largest by far, followed by Anders Gwin, a grey-scaled creature that was almost as famous as Mada. He'd been a legend in the industry even before Mada recruited him for his team. They'd worked together for several years. Next came Newac something-or-another. Adam knew him, too, but he could never recall his last name. Aliens seldom went by them, so he didn't really care. All he knew was that Newac was a wonder with weapons, almost as fast at the draw as Adam and nearly as strong. He also came from a heavy gravity world, although his race hadn't adapted so well to their native environment as had Humans. And last was Iroc Hans. He was the intellectual of the team, a wizard at electronic data gathering. He'd been an independent contractor for several Expansion governments until the Klin invasion. He'd only been part of Mada's team for about a year but had already proven himself invaluable. Since Adam had encountered the team before, he took note when news circulated around the office about some big bounty Mada and his team had recovered. They didn't do bodyguard work or hire themselves out as mercenaries. All they did was fugitive recovery, and primarily when there were big bucks on the line.

Adam still wondered what he could contribute to a team like this. So he asked, "How do you see this partnership working?"

"Very good question," Mada said. "First of all, for full disclosure, you need to know that my team and I were hired initially by Bandors Bank soon after the theft was discovered. They delayed reporting the incident to the authorities and the issuance of the warrant until we had a chance to investigate. That brought us to Kalicor, and we have been here for thirteen days. When the trail grew cold, the bank filed the report, and the warrant was issued, along with the reward."

"Yeah, that's information I wish I'd known before."

"It is why truly large bounties are seldom put on the Boards. Specialty teams, such as mine, are often called in ahead of time, and, as you know, we have a phenomenal success rate. But in this case, we have been stymied. The fact that you had already identified two of the prime suspects in only a few days is quite impressive." Mada smiled. "And if ever you wish to leave the employ of my friend Tidus, I would welcome you aboard my team. And you will not have to do bodyguard duties or serve as a hired gun any longer. Yes, I have been keeping track of your recent escapades. As I said last night, very impressive."

"Well, thanks. But now you think I can help with this case after the four of you have failed?"

"We have not failed!" Anders Gwin bellowed. "We are still on the hunt. As you know, some take longer than others."

"Of course, sorry," Adam said quickly. He respected the success rate of the team and didn't want to get off on the wrong foot. "I'm just wondering what I can bring to the table?"

"The table, as in meals and beverages?" Anders asked.

"No, he is referring to his contribution to the effort," Mada corrected. He was obviously better versed in Human-speak than were the others. "As I said, you found leads in three days that took us twenty days or so to develop, both here and on Tactori. Perhaps you have other leads not so well developed that we might assist you with."

"Well, there is one. You knew of the one here and also Ualic. But do you know about the one in Manisford?"

Mada looked at the rest of his team, focusing mainly on Iroc, the computer wizard. He shook his head.

"Tell me about it."

"Another Nija Falonmore, but the Nija, has an 'n' in it."

"What is an 'n?'"

"It's a letter in my native language. When you add it in a spot in the name, you get *Ninja*."

"And this is significant?"

"Possibly. You said there's a chance we're being tested to see if we're worthy of working with the thief. Well, in Human-speak, a *Ninja* is a type of stealth warrior, skilled and crafty and able to disappear at will. Kind of like our fugitive. There was a *Ninja* Falonmore in my research, and one of the Tactori liners landed not too far from her local address. It just seemed like a little too much coincidence."

"How would our fugitive know of the Human word?"

"I have no idea. But last night, you said you believed the original name was appropriated, stolen from someone else. It could be anyone. But if this is a test, then Ninja might be the perfect clue."

"Where is Manisford?" Mada asked Iroc.

Without checking his datapad, the alien said, "Kleinmock Province, seven hundred miles from here."

"Do you have the address?" Mada asked Adam.

"I do."

The bounty hunter boss grinned. "Then let us enjoy a first meal and then head that way. You say there is a spaceport nearby? I say we take separate ships; I know how protective our new friend here is of his personal space. With any luck, we will pass the thief's test and have the affair negotiated before time for the mid-meal. And thank you, my Human friend. You have vindicated my confidence in you, something my teammates were not as anxious to award. Welcome to the team, Adam Cain, and enjoy the meal. I am buying."

Adam thought this was getting off to a good start. He might enjoy working with Mada Niac. After all, Tidus had never bought him breakfast before, only a Diet Pepsi.

## 17

Kleinmock Province ended up encompassing a vast mountain range similar to the Alps, with stark granite pinnacles and glacier-filled valleys. The small spaceport was located at a lower elevation and nestled in the middle of a meadow with some of the greenest grass Adam had ever seen. The whole scene looked like something out of *The Sound of Music*. The area was popular with tourists, so the spaceport was compact and hosted an assortment of incredible private space yachts. If this is where the fugitive planned on settling down with her ill-gotten gains, she couldn't have done much better. But by now, Adam was convinced that Nija—or Ninja—Falonmore was an alias. He had no idea who the real thief would be.

Of course, this could also be another wild goose

chase. Mada and his team had scoured the planet for almost two weeks and come up empty. It would be a miracle if his offbeat lead actually turned into something.

Mada arranged for a large transport to be waiting for them, and they set out along a winding mountain road almost the second they touched down. The alien GPS system pinpointed Nija/Ninja's location to be at about eight-thousand-foot elevation and just off the main road.

Adam sat with his nose pressed against the glass of the front passenger seat—yes, he got the front seat while Anders drove, and Mada, Newac and Iroc sat in the back. The vehicle was large to accommodate the huge natives, so everyone had plenty of room.

The drive was breathtaking, climbing several thousand feet from the spaceport, with towering rock walls on one side of the road and vertigo-inducing drop-offs on the other. The higher peaks were covered in pristine white snow; this had to be the summer months on this part of Kalicor; otherwise, the whole place would be draped in a cloak of white.

Besides the incredible view, the air was as crisp as mint with a fragrance to match. Adam almost forgot he was on an alien world, and when he remembered, he made a mental note to keep Kalicor in mind. This would be a nice place to get away to now and then and commune with nature, even if it was alien nature.

The drive took about thirty minutes, and as they reached the turnoff, Newac began passing Xan-fi rifles to the team, including Adam. His eyes met Mada's, and the bounty hunter simply said, "Just in case we are *not* expected."

Anders had a datapad resting in a holder at his driver's station, watching a live satellite view of their approach. He zoomed out to see if there was any other activity on the road and, as they got closer, around the house. Everything was quiet.

The house was what Adam was hoping for; a log cabin of breathtaking proportions with towering raked windows facing a wide valley covered in evergreens. Life was ubiquitous in the galaxy, and carbon-based life tended to follow along more-or-less standard lines. Plants took in sunlight and produced chlorophyll which made trees, bushes and grass green, no matter what planet you were on. Each lifeform then fought for survival, if that meant developing nuclear weapons or simply reaching for the open sky to take in life-sustaining energy. Even more than the top-of-the-food-chain Prime life, plant life seemed universal from planet to planet, as if a single giant nursery had journeyed from world to world, landscaping the terrain like all the others.

Adam had once owned a log home off Highway 50 on the Nevada side of Lake Tahoe, so the mountains of Kalicor made him feel right at home. Perhaps it was the familiarity of the setting that made him homesick. Sure, this place was every bit what Earth was like, but it wasn't Earth. Knowing the truth put a slight damper on his emotions.

And then the car stopped, down the hill from the house and hidden within the woods. The team quickly disembarked, snapping Adam out of his musings. He now had a job to do, although, at the moment, he wasn't quite sure what it was. He'd led them to the house, and now it looked as though they were preparing for an assault. That was fine; Adam had done the same dozens of times. It was only an assumption that Nija would be waiting for them and anxious to get her freedom negotiated—for a price. If not, then a carload of bounty hunters showing up at your front door might evoke a more hostile greeting.

Adam marveled at the quiet efficiency of the team. No one had to be told what to do or where to station themselves. They, too, had been on dozens of raids of suspected fugitive hideouts. Since Adam wasn't an official member of the team, he chose to stay out of the way and remain at their six as they moved toward the house. He was a good backup but not part of the forward element.

Newac slipped around to the back. He was the best with a weapon, so he could cover more ground. Anders and Iroc took up flanking positions at the front door while Mada pulled down a flap on his shirt, revealing a yellow and red stripe. This was the accepted brand of a bounty hunter ... if people on Kalicor knew what the accepted brand meant. In the days of the Expansion, it was more recognized than it is now. Even though Mada wore a diffusion vest under his shirt, he was still taking a chance stepping up to the front door in plain view of any security cameras. And there would be cameras. That was something about the galaxy as a whole ... everyone had cameras.

If there was a doorbell, Mada didn't look for it. Instead, he rapped solidly on the wooden door.

A gravelly voice—either an AI or a person using a voicebox—came over hidden speakers.

"You are under surveillance, and defensive measures are active. The home is protected. State your business or leave the premises immediately."

Adam was hunched down behind a large spruce tree—an alien version of a spruce tree. He scanned the front façade of the home using the scope on the flash rifle. There were dozens of points where weapons could be hidden that covered the house effectively. There could even be remotes in the trees aimed back at the structure to catch anyone trying to hide, like Adam. He had no doubt the home could defend itself, even if no one was home.

"I am Mada Niac. I represent Bandors Bank. We are seeking an audience with Nija Falonmore. I believe you are expecting us."

That was ballsy, Adam thought. But was it any different than Adam running up to a door yesterday without a weapon drawn or wearing a diffusion shield? The only difference was he was sure he had the wrong house. This one checked all the boxes for someone who had just stolen twenty-five million energy credits.

"There will be a box on the right side as you enter. Place all your weapons within. I have scanners that can detect them, even hidden weapons. Yes, Mada Niac, I have been expecting you. You are here to negotiate, not to arrest. Keep that in mind. You will be covered every second you are within the home. I do not wish to harm you, and you do not wish to be harmed. Enter and conduct your business and then leave, and no one will be hurt."

Although the voice sounded as if it were computer generated—it undoubtedly was—the words seemed oddly familiar. Then the door clicked open, and the team was moving, even Newac from the back. Adam hurried out from behind the tree, not wanting to be left behind.

Mada and his people quickly and quietly relieved themselves of their weapons, which included a hell of a lot more than just the visible Xan-fis. Each of them carried at least half a dozen backups, from smaller energy weapons to an assortment of knives and even taser-like devices. Mada watched Adam follow suit, raising his eyebrows as Adam revealed his own cache of hidden weapons. He never left home without them.

The central feature of the home was the voluminous greatroom that dominated off to the left of the entry foyer. The view was incredible, but by now, Adam was beyond such distractions. He was on the job, and his senses heightened, like a cat on the prowl. He was looking for anything out of the ordinary, including smells and sounds.

One of the first things he noticed in the greatroom was a table with an active computer on it and a large monitor. There was a smaller unit off to the right, also on. They were expected, and this equipment was for them.

"Are you going to show yourself?" Mada asked.

Just then, a figure moved from the opposite side of the room, coming from an open portal that would lead to the bedrooms. The home was large on the outside, but most of the square footage was taken up with the greatroom.

The figure was slight, suggesting the form of a female. She was also cloaked from top to bottom in a black garment that seemed sheer in some ways but effectively hid her identity. She was also much shorter than a Kalicorean.

"Are you Nija Falonmore?" Mada asked.

"If you prefer, you can call me *Ninja*." The figure

seemed to turn toward Adam as she spoke, again in the disguised voice. Mada noticed.

"Introductions," Mada offered. "My team, Anders, Iroc and Newac. The other member is known as *The Human*."

Adam was thankful that Mada didn't reveal his name. It was becoming harder to keep his identity a secret as he gained more notoriety.

"I have been tracking your progress since you arrived on the planet. I am disappointed it took you so long to find me. I was told you are the best."

"It is a testament to your skill at remaining hidden. My Human friend provided the key to your location using the Ninja code you left. He says it is a Human word."

"I do my research. But I did not know there were Humans still this far out in the galaxy."

"He is a fellow bounty hunter, one of the best. He is assisting. I informed Bandors Bank of his joining the team. They seemed quite pleased. *The Human* is somewhat of a celebrity within my industry."

"I am just surprised to see a Human … in the flesh. It has been a while."

There it was again, that itchy feeling like something wasn't right. The words used and the cadence….

"Let us begin," Ninja ordered. "You may use the large terminal."

The figure of Ninja did not move farther into the

room, preferring to keep her back to the hallway leading from the greatroom.

Mada's agents stood in a line, appearing nervous without their weapons. But Mada was calm and collected as he swiftly moved to the monitor and sat down. He immediately started making entries on the alien keyboard, and within two minutes, a rotund, purple creature with four arms appeared on the screen. He was flanked by two other aliens, one tall, one short and each of different species.

"Champion Tanoric, as requested, I have located the one known as Nija Falonmore. She is with me. Is there anything you wish to say to her?"

The purple alien moved his wide lips, and the words that came through the monitor were nowhere synced with the words spoken. That was an issue with the universal translation bug. By now, Adam was so used to it that it had to be really bad for him to even notice. This time, he noticed.

"You have stolen from Bandors Bank, absconding with valuable depositor's credits. I am now making a formal demand for the immediate return of such stolen credits. If you oblige within the specified deadline, your criminal record and warrant for arrest will be expunged. If you do not agree to return the funds, then Mada Niac has the authorization to take you into custody for return to Tactori to face justice. However, you will receive a full pardon for return of the funds."

"Forgive me, Champion Tanoric, but I am more aware of how these negotiations take place than you give me credit for. In addition, I have full defenses which will prevent Mada Niac from apprehending me."

"If you do not oblige, then the warrant will stay in effect. If not Mada Niac and his team, then there will be others."

"If you will allow me," Mada spoke up. "There is a solution to this impasse; there always is. To begin, even if we are able to arrest Nija Falonmore, there is no guarantee that any of the stolen funds will be recovered. Therefore, I propose a settlement offer, a smaller amount that the bank will receive now, a guarantee of at least a partial return of the lost funds.."

Adam was amused with the bankers as they began discussing things out of range of the camera's microphone. He got the feeling that this was all rehearsed, possibly a play that had to be performed for the benefit of auditors or shareholders. Adam could see how he would have completely screwed this up. First of all, he didn't have the link number for the bigwigs at Bandors Bank.

"A reasonable settlement would be twenty million of the twenty-five million taken," said the four-armed creature. "Even though that will be insulting to the shareholders to allow a commission of five million for stealing from us, we will accept that for the timely return of the balance."

"Unacceptable," Nija stated firmly, not even giving it a moment of consideration. "We can reverse those numbers. I will return five million."

The purple being laughed, joined by the others in the room with him. "That is absurd, that is insulting. You stole from us!" That didn't sound rehearsed.

"Again, if I may," said Mada. "I have sat through several of these negotiations, and I know it is not unreasonable to accept fifty percent as a settlement, twelve point five million credits." He looked at the cloaked figure. "That still leaves an impressive sum. And you did commit a crime."

The bankers remained quiet. They seemed okay with fifty percent. Hell, so was Adam. He didn't know what recovery percentage Mada would negotiate, but whatever it was, it was going to be a huge payday.

"Unacceptable."

"Very well then—" Mada stammered to silence, then quickly turned away from the screen and glared at the cloaked female. "Unacceptable?" He seemed genuinely caught off guard by her proclamation.

"I will not pay more than ten million. If you do not accept that, then these negotiations are at an end. I will take my chances that you will not find me. The only reason you found me this time was because I let you. I fear not future hunters. I'm better than they are."

Mada stared at her for a moment in silence before turning reluctantly back to the screen. "The offer is ten million," he recited blandly. "And I will be asking for a twenty-percent recovery fee."

Adam batted his eyes. That was two million, and with Starfire getting half. There was the million-credit bounty as advertised. And what, it took four days, including travel time. Adam could get used to working on these kinds of deals.

The bankers conferred again before purple skin came back, shaking his head. "Twenty percent is too high. With a recovery of only ten million, we will only pay fifteen percent."

Fifteen percent. Adam shrugged. That was still seven hundred fifty thousand credits for Starfire. Thirty percent of that would be ….

He was still working out his commission when Mada accepted the terms. He looked to Nija.

"Acceptable."

"Good. Now, remove the warrant and issue the forgiveness," he said to the bankers.

Champion Tanoric—Adam didn't know if Champion was his title or his first name—nodded and then looked back into the camera. "Funds to be delivered no later than six standard days from now to our headquarters on Tactori. Funds shall be in physical chips." It sounded to Adam as if he were reading off a cue card. "Once the documents have been cleared and possession secured, it will become the responsibility of Mada Niac and his team to deliver said funds. Any delay or other interference will be met with the harshest of response."

"And this will absolve me of all consequences regarding the theft and stop all collection proceedings," Nija stated.

"Upon the release of the documents, yes," said Tanoric.

"Agreed," said Nija.

"Agreed," said Mada.

Adam knew the negotiations were being recorded and would serve as legal notice of the terms.

Tanoric nodded. "It is done. Verify."

Mada slipped over to the second computer. A moment later: "Verified. The warrant has disappeared from the Boards, and the criminal record of Nija Falonmore has been expunged."

"Six days, Mada," Tanoric reaffirmed.

"Understood." He kept a straight face, hiding any emotion surrounding the transaction. In fact, he almost looked mad.

"It was a pleasure doing business with you," Nija announced from across the room. Tanoric and the others heard it. They responded by cutting the link.

## 18

Mada swung the chair around until he faced Nija.

"I suppose you already have the *ten* million counted out."

He almost sounded rude. Apparently, he didn't like having his negotiations messed with, especially by a damn thief. And it also cost him two-hundred and fifty thousand credits. More than that. Mada thought she was going to settle for twelve-point-five and with a twenty percent recovery fee. That math Adam could do in his head. That was two and a half million. And half of that was one-point-two-five. Hell, she'd also cost Adam a sizable chunk of change.

"I have it ready. It is behind the seat to your left."

"Pretty sure of yourself, are you not?" Mada asked.

"It is my money. I will part with only as much as I'm willing."

Mada nodded to Anders, who went to the chair and found the case. It was a box like a packing storage crate, two feet tall by three long and a foot and a half wide. He slid the box over so all could see and then pulled off the lid. It was filled to the brim with thousands of shiny new energy chips about the size of a credit card from Earth. From what Adam could see, most or all were green, signifying twenty-thousand credit denomination, the largest made. This was the new currency of the galaxy, replacing Juirean credits as legal tender on over eight thousand Prime worlds. And rather than being backed by the good faith of the Juirean Expansion, these were covered by interest in energy stocks, such as for cold fusion reactors, gravity generators and other assorted producers. At one time, ten million JCs wasn't a lot. But with the changeover after the invasion, ten million energy credits were worth in the neighborhood of fifty million old Juirean credits. This was a big deal.

"Adam, could you do the honors?"

Adam jumped at the sound of his name. At least Mada hadn't spoken his last name.

"What?"

"The box. It is quite heavy. But not for a Human."

Adam almost snickered. Almost. He strode up to the imposing alien figure of Anders Gwin. He towered over the six-foot-tall Human, and yet it was Adam who was tasked with hauling the treasure out of the house. It was too heavy for any of the aliens to lift.

"If someone could recover my weapons on the way out, I would appreciate it."

Adam bent at the knees and grabbed the handles. Then he lifted. For a moment, nothing happened, not until he tried a little harder. Now the box came off the ground, barely. He struggled with the case until he had it up to his belt. He wedged it against the strap, using his belly to help support the weight.

*Damn, this thing must weigh two hundred pounds, Earth pounds*, Adam thought as he struggled toward the door. Iroc had the courtesy to open the door for him. But Adam wasn't about to ask for help. He was *The Human*, super-alien. And he was about a foot or two shorter than all the other team members. The fact that Mada knew about Humans' superior strength was telling, and yes, none of his team would have been able to get the box more than a couple of inches off the floor, not even the heavy-worlder Iroc.

Adam was sweating like a pig by the time he lugged the box of ten million credits to the car, which was down the hill—luckily—but still about a quarter of a mile away from the house. Anders, Iroc and Newac came with him bringing his weapons, leaving Mada alone with the former fugitive. Perhaps there was a little side deal taking place. That was fine. He'd done a better job than Adam would have. It pays to have experience. However, Adam now knew another side of the bounty hunting business, one that paid better and where you got invited into the home of the fugitive. He might consider future jobs like this.

He slid the box into the back of the transport and then sat on the bumper to catch his breath. Besides the sheer weight, the house was at about eight-thousand-foot elevation, so the air was thinner here. Sure, he was stronger than most, but he still had his limits.

He welcomed the reprieve. The other three members of the team stood off to the side, passing a smokestick between themselves. They didn't offer Adam a hit. That was fine. He needed time for his muscles and lungs to recover, and his panting and sweat were embarrassing. Even so, he would have liked to see any of them do what he just did.

For their part, the team seemed to be in a good mood, at least better than Mada during the negotiations. They should be; they had another successful—successful what? It wasn't really a fugitive recovery, now was it? But they did recover some of the stolen money. That counted for something. And it was all thanks to Adam thinking outside of the box and linking *Ninja* with *Nija*. It wasn't that much of a stretch.

But Mada was pissed off. Adam wondered if he was inside the house chewing out Nija for screwing with his negotiations. He wouldn't put it past him.

Soon, Mada joined them, and he didn't say much as he climbed into the passenger seat in the front, seemingly lost in thought. His forehead was furrowed, and his eyes clouded. He'd just closed another large bounty, and instead of enjoying the moment as the others were, he was downright morose.

Adam was demoted and relegated to one of the back seats. *So be it*, Adam thought. He'd served his purpose, so he didn't have to be treated special anymore. Now, it was just a matter of delivering the money to the bank. Adam wondered if he would be going to Tactori with them. How would he get paid if he didn't? Did he trust Mada enough to send Tidus their share? The answer was no. Adam didn't trust anyone that much.

## 19

Anders was in the driver's seat and taking them back down the mountain. As before, Adam had a chance to marvel at the spectacular scenery, which again reminded him of the snow-capped mountains around his beloved Lake Tahoe. Perhaps with his share of the bounty, he could take the time to return to Earth, at least for a visit. There would be no need to let anyone know he was coming; that would only risk the possibility of the media finding out. And then it would be the same old thing: questions about his age and even if he was indeed the real Adam Cain. It had happened before; it would happen again.

He changed his mind. If he couldn't go back to Earth, he could at least come back to Kalicor, and just in time for the first snowfall of the season. Perhaps the aliens even skied. It had been years since he'd hit the slopes, but he was sure that with his new body—and in alien gravity—he could tear up some moguls. He'd check if there were any resorts in the area once he got back to the spaceport.

Adam was suddenly thrown against the window glass as the transport spun to its left and screeched to a halt. Recovering with a bloody nose, Adam looked out the window to see a phalanx of three other vehicles blocking the road. An assortment of armed and armored aliens hid behind the cars as another stood holding a shoulder-fired bolt cannon on Adam's car. Newac had his Xan-fi pointed out the window, with the other two bounty hunters—Anders and Iroc—only a second behind. They'd brought back Adam's weapons to the car, but he'd left them in the back with the box of energy credits.

"Hold!" Mada shouted, filling the inside of the car with a domineering command. Everyone froze. "Do not provoke them."

*Yeah, please don't,* Adam thought. If the cannon bolt hit the car, they'd be cleaning energy credits off the mountain for months, along with their blood.

With his arms at his side, Mada exited the vehicle. Slowly, the rest of the team joined him, including Adam. They brought their Xan-fis but immediately set them on the road at their feet.

There were eight of the raiders, and four of them

rushed in and took the weapons as the other four—including the guy with the flash cannon—covered them. Then they rushed to the back of the car and opened the hatch. They didn't remove the box; instead, one of them furtively nodded at Mada. Adam noticed while the other three bounty hunters were focused on the aliens with the guns.

Mada stepped to the side and closer to the raiders. Adam continued to stare, meeting Mada's eyes. The huge alien grinned. Then a raider handed Mada his MK-17. Mada's full team now saw what happened. Mouths fell open in questioning disbelief.

"Sorry, my friends," Mada said with a smirk. "But the plan calls for sacrifices to make it convincing."

And then he fired, not waiting for the targeting computer to lock on. Adam had been looking at the barrel of the weapon when it went off and was temporarily blinded by the brilliant flash. Still, out the corner of his eye, he saw first Newac, then Anders, then Iroc go down from what Adam knew to be Level-1 bolts. His vision cleared enough to see Mada's satisfied look as he turned the weapon on Adam.

"And you, Mr. Cain. I appreciate your contribution to the operation. You played your part perfectly." And then he pulled the trigger.

Adam was flung back by the intense force of the bolt striking his chest center mass. He wasn't wearing a diffusion vest like the others, so the bolt was a kill shot.

For the others, Mada aimed for their unprotected heads, creating a horrific scene like something out of the *Friday the Thirteenth* movies. Adam ended up on his stomach, his chest on fire as intense spasms of electricity tore through his body. He continued to twitch, just as the headless corpses of the others did, yet unlike the others, Adam wasn't dead. Not yet.

His mind was a jumble, and his vision was that from the inside of a spin dryer. His breathing was shallow, with the rising and falling of his smoldering chest hidden by the electrical spasms. He heard the crunching of gravel as Mada made the rounds of his handiwork. Adam did his best to play dead, even as he used the spasms to cock his head slightly so he could look out at the gathering of henchmen around the bounty hunter boss.

"Load these three in the transport," he said. "I will need them as proof of The Human's treachery."

"And him?" someone asked.

"His body must not be found. Toss it over the cliff. Let the wild animals feast on his carcass. And when you are done with that, take your team and return to the residence. There has been a change in the plan, and a loose end must be tended to. Find the rest of the credits and then dispose of her body as you did with the Human. And a word of caution: She, too, is a Human, so beware. The defenses of the home are a myth, so you will have no problem gaining entrance.

All the same, she is a Human, and they can be very unpredictable. I will meet you at the spaceport when you are done. Now, get it over with."

Adam watched as Mada took a deep breath and turned sideways to the goon, drawing a line with his hand across his side and up under his left arm. "Along here. And please, a Level-2. I would not want to join my colleagues, but it must be convincing. After that, tend to your tasks."

The alien stepped back from Mada, aimed his MK-17, and fired. It was a glancing hit, but on an alien, even a Level-2 bolt is lethal. Mada spun around and dropped to his knees, grimacing in pain. The side of his shirt was burnt off, with the skin underneath already blistering. He nearly passed out but managed to recover, climbing unsteadily to his feet.

"*Drasen-mok!* That hurt!" he groaned. Then he looked at his wound, nodding approvingly. "That should work. Now, go. Bring the rest of the credits to the spaceport. Judge the delivery by the number of authorities around my vessel."

Mada staggered to the transport and struggled to climb into the driver's seat while rough hands took hold of Adam's body and lifted him off the road. He was helpless as he was carried toward the right side of the road. Then with no hesitation, Adam Cain was unceremoniously tossed down the cliff as if the aliens were taking out the trash.

## 20

Adam was in no condition to marvel at the sensation of flight as he flew through the air. And then he hit something—a branch—and then a *lot* of branches. His limp body tumbled and twisted, slapped by countless pine needles and bouncing through an assortment of native trees. He hit hard against a solid object that didn't give way and ricocheted off at a radical angle before landing on a bed of rounded rocks.

He may have lost consciousness—he wasn't sure—but he was suddenly aware of where he was. His body still twitched from the electricity coursing through his body, and he knew it would eventually fry his brain, and he would die. The wound on his chest wouldn't do it, but the electricity would.

Adam had no idea how shattered his body was; he

couldn't feel anything beyond the excruciating jolts of energy attacking his body. They weren't letting up; if anything, they were growing stronger.

Then Adam heard the sound of a nearby river or stream. With his vision racked by spasms, he could barely make out his surroundings, but he knew the sound was coming from his right. He was on his stomach, his face pressed against the cold rocks of the shoreline. Through blurred vision, he saw the color shift where the river began. It was only a few feet away.

Again, not knowing if every bone in his body was broken, he tried to move. He felt a strangeness in his body, a confusion that was both painful and stimulating. Was this his body injecting him was an abundance of adrenaline? Was it *willing* him to move?

He experimented with his legs checking to see if he had control of his limbs. He felt a foot brace against a stone. He pushed. His body began to slide on the smooth yet uneven surface. Adam moved his feet again, finding another purchase. He had no idea if what he was feeling was the onset of shock or if the pain had simply overwhelmed his senses. Either way, he continued to move, an inch or two at a time.

He felt a cold drop on his face and listened as the sound of the water seemed to smother him. Adam twisted his head. He moved his right arm, lifting it slightly before giving up and letting it fall. The tips of his fingers reached the water.

And that's when an explosion of sparks flew out of his body and along the shoreline. It was like a toaster being thrown into a tub of water, but instead of the current being drawn from the power grid, the sparks were coming from Adam's overcharged body.

In only a few seconds, nearly all of the excess electricity had been pulled from him. Now, not only the angry wound in the center of his chest was smoking, but so was the rest of his body. He could smell his burning flesh and hair, and he puked, spilling even more foul odor onto the riverbank. Gone was the minty freshness of the mountain landscape.

With the electrical current drained from his body, Adam felt much better. He rolled over and lay on his back, his eyes closed against the harsh glare of midday on Kalicor. He breathed as steady as possible, feeling his heart still struggling to get back into rhythm. He was alive; that much he knew. But what condition he was in was a mystery.

After a few minutes, Adam began to feel the cold of the rocks against his back. That was a good sign. He could feel them from his head to his feet, meaning he had sensations along his entire body. Next, he tested his limbs, lifting them a little and twisting his ankles. There was pain, but nothing sharp and penetrating. He was bruised and battered, but nothing seemed to be broken.

He opened his eyes and looked up along the craggy

length of the rock wall from the road above to the river below. There were a number of tall evergreens growing along the cliff, and fortunately, he'd been tossed into the middle of a thick grove. It was a testament to his Human bone density and thick muscles that nothing was broken. He also had to give credit to the lower gravity of Kalicor. The trees he crashed through weren't as rigid or dense as those on Earth. The branches broke more readily; at least some did. Adam was still a mess, but he would heal. Already the pain was subsiding as his cloning feature was kicking into high gear. Since his death, this was probably the closest he'd come to dying again. His body knew it and was working overtime to correct the damage.

Adam chuckled—and yes, it hurt like hell. The thought had hit him the cloning gods expected only perfect results at the end of the process, and any abnormalities along the way had to be immediately addressed. Because of that, Adam was already feeling the effects of the narcotic euphoria he'd experienced before, but this time it came sooner and with more intensity. Yeah, he'd come close to dying, but his body was not about to give up on him.

Ten minutes, an hour—Adam didn't know—he lay there. Soon he felt strong enough to move, to get off the cold rocks that were now beginning to make his back hurt and his joints stiffen. If it wasn't one thing, it was another.

Even as he got to his feet, his mind was racing, recalling what had just happened and what he'd heard and seen from Mada Niac.

Mada killed his team ... and he was going to blame Adam for it. He was going to take the ten million credits and accuse Adam of stealing, And, of course, Adam wouldn't be alive to dispute the story.

Yeah, well fuck you, Mada Niac," Adam said aloud —to no one.

And then he remembered more. This memory made him shake his head in disgust. He should have known; all the signs were there. Ninja Falonmore—or whatever her name was—is a Human. Then he snorted. More correctly, *was* a Human, he thought. She's probably lying at the bottom of a ravine by now, just like Adam.

Even so, there might be a car at the house or a way to make a call. It was the only play he had. By now, Mada would have spread the lie that Adam killed the team and then took off with the money. And only Mada miraculously survived to tell the tale after suffering a near-fatal wound himself. Adam needed to call Tidus. He needed a way out of this, and the Juirean was the only friend Adam had within a hundred light-years. That thought was depressing.

Gingerly making his way over the river rocks and to the cliff wall, Adam surveyed the outcroppings for a path back to the road two hundred feet above. Every joint in his body ached, including his ankles and knees, elbows and wrists, everything he would need to climb the wall. Fortunately, there wasn't a lot of loose rock. The roadway was cut out of solid rock, and Adam found a virtual stairway going up the slope. There were a lot of switchbacks and scary moments as he almost met the rocky riverbank again, but eventually, he crested the summit and climbed over the rail guard along the road.

If he recalled accurately, they'd only gone a couple of miles down the mountain when the ambush took place. Still, a two-mile hike on an incline was torture. Besides that, Adam ducked for cover every time he heard a car coming down the road. It could be the henchmen returning from their latest assassination. Then Adam corrected himself. They didn't assassinate Mada's team—he did. Whether that made a difference or not, he wasn't sure. But to Adam, it was a really shitty thing to do.

And that's when Adam smelled smoke.

## 21

Callie Morrison—AKA Ninja Falonmore—was steaming mad. How dare that asshole Mada browbeat her like that. This *was* her plan; all he did was provide the cover.

Hell, by all rights, she could have accepted the twenty-mill buy-off and kept the five. But that wouldn't have been convincing enough. Hell, she had done enough of these stings to know what would have the most effect. Mada was new to her side of the table. Sure, he had a shitload of experience in dealing with people like her that he could second guess them. But she had that certain something that people called a *gift*. She knew she could press for more, and she'd get it.

Of course, Mada was right. None of this really mattered. It was just a game she was playing to see if she could get away with it. They were going to get all the money in the end, and free and clear, thanks to the patsy.

What she hadn't planned on was that the patsy would be a Human.

That threw her for a loop. Hell, she hadn't seen another Human in over a year. And, sure, being in her line of work, she'd heard of the one they called *The Human*. What a pompous windbag! Oh, look at me, I'm *THE* Human. As if he was the only Human left in the galaxy. What a jerk. Still, she felt bad that one of her kind was going to take the fall. She laughed. The fall. She knew what Mada was planning for the body of the patsy. That's why she picked this picturesque setting in the first place.

And damn, was it picturesque. At first, she picked Kalicor because the natives looked remarkably like Humans. A few prosthetics on the ears to make her look like an elf, then a little more flesh on the jowls and lifts in her shoes, and she could pass for a Kalicorean. Depending on how the rest of the caper played out, she might consider coming back here again, maybe doing some skiing. She used to be pretty good at it.

But first, she had to pack. Mada would tell his story about the theft—the original theft—and the negotiations with the bank. Technically, she was in the clear, but she wasn't going to take any chances. Besides, she'd just stiffed Mada out of two and a half million credits. That didn't go over very well with the alien. She laughed. But it sure was fun. She was supposed to accept the twelve five, giving each of them an even split. He was to leave with his half and blame the patsy for stealing it, and she'd be free and clear with the other half. No need to meet up again.

That was what pissed him off so much when she didn't accept the offer. But hey, she felt she deserved the lion's share of the booty. After all, it was her caper in the first place, and she'd spent three damn months working in that stinking alien bank to make it happen. Not Mada.

But now she had to leave. Mada may or may not accept his loss. He said he would after his team left the house. But she couldn't be sure. He was new to being a criminal, and if he was willing to kill his long-term and loyal team for a measly twelve-point-five mill, he might kill her—a stranger—to get the rest he thought was owed him.

*Screw the alien! That will teach him to partner with a Human.*

And then an alarm softly chimed.

She tensed. The story about the elaborate security features of the house had mostly been bullshit. Mostly. She still had a proximity alarm set at the property's perimeter. She rushed to the monitor to see if it was simply an animal, a native deer perhaps.

"Fuck," she breathed. "That's no deer."

On the monitor, she saw four, no five—hell, there

were eight of them—all aliens and moving stealthily through the woods toward the house. They carried Xan-fis, and one even had the equivalent of an alien RPG, although this rocket-propelled grenade launcher fired cannon bolts.

She'd run this scenario through her head a dozen times or more. Callie had to be prepared if a random bounty hunter chanced upon her location before Mada arrived. But she hadn't counted on eight assailants. She headed to a back room where she kept the armory. Yes, Callie Morrison had an armory. It consisted of mainly alien weaponry—which was replaceable—along with a small cache of Human ballistics. But her prized possession was an old M1A4 assault rifle, the kind the special forces once used back on Earth. The weapon had belonged to her grandfather, and she'd brought it with her into the galaxy. She never left home without it.

But now she had a dilemma. She had fifteen million credits worth of plastic chips in another room and a transport out back. She needed time to load the money, along with her personal belongings. She wouldn't have time to do that before the stormtroopers got to the house.

Her M1A4 had more range than did the alien bolt launchers, so that gave her an advantage. She could try to take them out at a distance. But could she clear all eight of them? She would have to if she was to have time to get the money and run.

Dammit, she should have already had it loaded. But Mada advised against that, thinking one of his agents might happen upon the car and check it out. Now she was pissed for listening to him.

She would have to fight them off. Callie shrugged. *Oh, well,* she thought. *It's not like I've never killed an alien before.*

---

She slipped out the back door before the aliens got close enough to notice. She figured she'd have more latitude being out in the forest. She had the rifle and four extra magazines, giving her plenty of firepower. Take a position, waste a couple of baddies, and then shift to another position and take out some more. She'd have to keep moving, but as she entered the tree line at the side of the house, she was almost giddy. This could be fun.

She knew the lay of the land, and the aliens didn't. They were coming up the main road in double two-by-two cover positions, two covering on each side of the road while two moved forward about ten feet at a time. This type of hopscotch maneuver was slow, and it gave Callie time to get to her position about two hundred yards out. She lay on the soft pine needle mat below a tree and sited her first targets. They lined up fairly well, giving her a chance at a *Quigley*—taking two targets out with a single shot. But she didn't have the right caliber ammo for that. She'd have to settle for two quick shots. Once that happened, the enemy would scatter, making her job demonstrably harder. Then it would become a game of cat and mouse.

Flicking off the safety, Callie lined up on the first target, then shifted to the second, getting a feel for the motion. Then she held her breath and pulled the trigger.

The loud report echoed through the mountains, made more prominent by the immediate second shot. Both targets dropped like bags of wet cement.

Callie was on the move, dodging around trees and diving into gullies, moving to flank the alien force. As expected, they didn't respond at first to the sound of the assault rifle, unfamiliar with the blast of a ballistic weapon. But when their comrades keeled over dead, they quickly put two and two together. Flash bolts erupted, firing at—who knew? And that was dangerous. She was out of range of the bolts, but the white-hot projectiles immediately torched wherever they impacted, setting the pine needles on fire.

The scattered fires cut off part of her movement, steering her closer to the road where there was less cover. She dropped to her belly again and sighted another of the advancing aliens. She dropped him with another echoing explosion.

But now, the enemy was better able to identify the

direction of the sound, reacting to the first blast and ignoring all the later echoes. They weren't the best field operators, but they learned quickly.

What bothered Callie was the use of flash bolts in a forest. Surely they knew that setting everything ablaze was counterproductive. She took cover again and assessed the surrounding flames as they quickly grew, going so far as to use a horrible Sean Connery accent to bastardize the famous line from *The Hunt for Red October*. "Some things in here don't respond well to flash bolts."

She popped out from behind a tree and took out another unsuspecting alien, taking her count to four out of eight. But that wasn't good enough. The front part of the forest leading to the main road was rapidly being consumed by fire. Even if she killed the last four, she needed to load the chips and get the hell out of there. She could do it, but she had to hurry.

She made it back to the house, hoping that the fire and confusion in the forest would convince the remaining aliens that she was still out there and not in the house. She shouldered the M1A4 and made for the bedroom where the money was stored. It was a lot, four heavy crates. She'd watched the other Human try to haul one of these things out the door, and she wasn't nearly as strong as he was. She resorted to dragging a crate across the tile floor. It worked but took longer than she had hoped. She secured the lid so it wouldn't come open and then rolled the crate into the trunk of her car before returning to the room for another crate.

She could see the flames dancing up the towering trees outside the house, now only feet away. And then the front door to the house blew open, having been struck by a flash cannon bolt. Callie was in the greatroom at the time, dragging the second crate toward the back. The concussion threw her toward the kitchen. It also sent the crate flying and spraying green energy credits across the greatroom.

"No!" she yelled as she whipped the rifle off her back. She sprayed the front door, catching the first aliens as they stormed the building. One went down while the other ducked back out.

Five down.

But now she'd lost a crate of chips. She headed for the bedroom again, her ears ringing from the concussion from the cannon bolt. Hopefully, she'd taken out the shooter. If not—

The second cannon bolt streaked through the air, appearing as a beam rather than a single ball of energy. Fortunately, it was aimed such that it didn't strike anything in the house until it impacted the rear wall. Then it exploded.

Callie was in the bedroom, and the blast rocked the house enough to knock her off her feet. She looked at the remaining two crates of chips, approximately eight million worth. She wouldn't be able to get them out.

She would have to settle for four million already in the car.

"Fuck, fuck, fuck," she yelled as she ran out of the bedroom and down the corridor to the greatroom, ready to shoot anything that moved.

Flames were whipping up the sides of the magnificent windows that made up a full wall of the home. And then the glass shattered, raining down on her. She ducked for cover under the dining table, only to be narrowly missed by a flash bolt coming from the front door. She lay over on her side and opened up, having to stop at a point to snap in another magazine. Just as she was taking aim again, two of the remaining aliens were thrown into the room, their backs a blaze by the impact of two quick flash bolts. Then the third stepped in. He had his back to Callie, firing at something—or someone—outside the front door. And then he took a bolt to the chest.

That was eight. But now she had this mysterious shooter to contend with.

"You, inside the house, don't shoot!"

"Who are you?"

"I'm the other Human."

"Bullshit! You're dead."

"Not this time."

Callie shook her head. That wasn't the response she expected.

"Mada was supposed to kill you."

"He tried, but it didn't take."

All right, she thought. This was *The Human*; no doubt about it. He talked like a Human, which was unique in the galaxy.

"Okay, I won't shoot … if you don't."

The Xan-fi rifle flew through the air and landed on the tile floor, sliding almost all the way to Callie. She came out from under the table just as what was left of the person known as *The Human* came through the door.

"I thought you said he *didn't* kill you. You could've fooled me."

The man was still smoldering from top to bottom. She didn't know if this was from the fire outside or from the bolt wound to his chest. His clothing was torn to shreds, and there didn't seem to be a part of his body that wasn't covered in blood.

"Damn, are you sure you survived?"

"I'm not so sure." He looked around at the carnage in the house and at the flames that were rapidly consuming everything. "I could say the same about you. Lucky I found a spare Xan-fi lying next to an alien with a 7.26 round shot cleanly through his head."

"You know your weapons, Mr. Human, sir."

"Occupational hazard."

"Former military on Earth?"

"Yep. And you?"

"Same. Seems like a lifetime ago."

"For me, it was."

Callie shook her head again. "All right, enough chit-chat. I'm heading out the back. It was nice talking to you, but as you can see, we can't stay here."

Just then, the back wall of the house caved in. Callie was hit by a burning timber and knocked into the greatroom. She was groggy, barely conscious.

The other Human was at her side a moment later. He hoisted her into his arms, groaning as he did so—hey, she wasn't that heavy—and began carrying her to the front door.

"No, wait! We can't leave," she cried out.

"No choice, sweetheart."

"But the money!"

"Where is it?"

"In the car in the back."

"We can't get to it through the house. We'll have to go around the side."

"Put me down!" Callie yelled once they were out the door.

The man smiled—it was a nice smile—with his teeth being about the only part of his body that wasn't covered in blood. And under it all, he was cute. Hell, even Quasimodo would be cute to Callie. At least he was Human. It had been a while.

He set her down. "And here I was enjoying the intimacy,"

She was steadier now and led the pair to the side of the house, only to be thrown back by a wall of fire.

"The other way!" she cried.

But then that way was blocked, too. The two Humans ran out into the road at the front of the house and looked back as the entire structure was now consumed by flames. Callie was crestfallen. It was gone, all of it. Six months of planning and six months of execution. A full year and nothing to show for it.

"C'mon, Ninja, we gotta go," the man said tenderly.

Callie was staring at the burning house, oblivious to the growing heat. Perhaps the tears streaming down her face cooled her skin enough, so she didn't care.

But then a swift tug on her arm got her moving. She raced down the road, which was about the only place clear of flames. Luckily, no wind was blowing, so the flames only climbed up at the moment. Even so, the forest was engulfed, and soon, so would half the mountain.

She ran, surprisingly outpacing the taller, stronger man. But then she slowed, allowing his battered body to catch up. He seemed to appreciate the gesture.

Once they reached the main road heading down the mountain, they found a little reprieve. The flames were climbing up the mountain, not down it. Callie knew that alien fire-fighting technology was better than Human tech—at least the tech before Earth entered the galaxy. Flying craft would soon appear and drop fire canceling chemicals that would make short work of the fire. And maybe someday, as workers sifted through the remains of a once magnificent log home, they'll find hardened puddles of melted plastic ... about fifteen million credits worth of melted plastic.

## 22

"Callie Morrison," the woman said after she and Adam had hiked about a mile down the hill.

"Adam Cain," he blurted without thinking. It was funny how natural it felt to be next to another Human. It had been a while.

"Bullshit," Callie said with no humor or anger. She was too depressed to care.

"Why bullshit?"

"Because he's dead. Probably died of old age. Hell, he was a legend when I was a kid. But nice try. What's your real name?"

"Would you believe Roy Rogers? Yippie-kay-yay—"

"No, I wouldn't believe that, either. Fine, have it

your way, asshole. But I'm not going to call you 'The Human,' or even *Humie* for short."

"I kinda like Humie. No one has ever called me that before."

"I've been called that ... and I hate it."

"Watch out; someone's coming." Adam took Callie by the arm and pulled her into the forest at the side of the road. A train of emergency vehicles screamed up the road, heading for the fire. Assuming Mada had already reported the killings—and blamed them on Adam, he didn't want to take a chance making contact with ... well, anyone.

After the cars and trucks raced by, they resumed the walk.

Callie looked over at him; he was still hobbling but not as bad as before.

"What the hell happened to you?"

He told her.

She laughed.

"I don't think it's that funny."

"I do! They threw you over a fucking cliff! Nice."

"I almost died."

"It will help build character; that's what my granddad used to say."

"Almost dying builds character?"

"It allows a person to examine their life's choices, and then to make adjustments along the way, he used to say."

Adam couldn't argue with that. Having died once already did reset his priorities. But he didn't tell Callie that.

"So, you're pretty handy with an old M1A4," he said instead. "Where did you learn that?"

"You recognized the weapon—fuck, that was lost in the fire, too! That was my grandfather's. He was a SEAL, special forces. Do you know what that is … or was. They don't have them anymore."

"I've heard of them. And I'm familiar with older Earth weapons."

"My granddad taught me how to shoot, and then I spent four years in the Marines, Force Recon."

"Green or Black?"

Callie looked at Adam and raised her eyebrows. "You really do know your stuff."

"I read a lot."

"I started Green but then spent the last year in Black. We mainly specialized in ship boardings—spaceships, of course. It was a blast, but then I got injured."

"What happened?"

"Caught some shrapnel in the leg. It knocked me down for a while, long enough for me to decide to muster out after my first term. But, damn, I loved being in space. At least at that time. I'm telling ya, things have changed."

"I hear you. Where were you during the invasion?"

"Running scams in the Kidis Frontier. Ever been there?"

Adam nodded.

Callie continued. "It didn't get hit as bad, so I was pretty much isolated. And then, all of a sudden, it ended. Strange, but then it left the galaxy all fucked up." She smiled. It was a nice smile. "Of course, it left a target-rich environment for people like me … and you tracking people like me. Ain't we a pair. Two sides of the same coin."

"You could say that. So, how did you and Mada get hooked up?"

"He tracked me down, of course, but instead of turning me in, we began working a few deals together. When I thought of the Bandors Bank job, it was right up his alley. I needed an inside guy, and he was it. He jumped at the chance." She snickered again. "I really pissed him off when I didn't take the twelve-five. That was our deal; he'd get half, and I'd get half. But fuck him. That's what I say." She looked over at Adam and his battered and bruised body. "I'm sorry it was you who got set up to take the fall. I didn't know."

"It's cool. I didn't know you were a Human, either."

"Would it have changed things?"

He pursed his lips. "Probably not. I've known some real bastards in my life who were Humans; in fact, some of the *biggest*."

"We do have a knack for being bastards, don't we?"

Callie was walking with purpose. It was eight miles down the mountain from the cabin to the spaceport, and she seemed anxious to get there. Not so much for Adam. He knew what would be waiting for him.

"What are you going to do when we get to town?" Adam asked. "Mada will know you survived when none of his team return. And he's probably already reported the killings and the theft and blamed them on me. Hell, you may even be in the story by now. He has to make some excuse to the bank why he lost the money, and having a couple of bastard Humans colluding together only adds to the fantasy."

"Fuck 'em all," she said. "I have a ship at the spaceport that no one knows about; a little speeder in a private hanger. I'm getting in it and heading for the other side of the galaxy." She took a furtive glance at Adam. "If you want, I could drop you somewhere."

"I have my own—*ah, shit!*"

"What?"

"If I stole the money, I'd be off the planet by now."

"Yeah?"

"So, that means Mada has to get rid of my ship. It's at the spaceport. We took separate spaceships coming here. The *Arieel* is my home. Everything I have is onboard."

"Well, everything I owned was in the house that

just burnt to the ground, including fifteen million in energy credits."

"Sounds like we're both up shit's creek."

Callie nodded, invoking a laugh from Adam.

"What?"

"It's just a relief talking to someone I don't have to explain every other word to."

Now Callie snickered. "You got that right. Fucking aliens."

Yeah, the lady had definitely been in the service, that's for sure, Adam thought. Although she'd been in the Marines, she swore like a Sailor. Still, it was refreshing having a conversation with another Human. The past three years had been tough.

They walked in silence for another two miles.

"You know, we can't let Mada get away with this," Adam said out of the blue. He'd been thinking hard for the last thirty minutes.

"Sorry, sweetheart, but he already has."

"Has he?"

She looked cockeyed at him. "I guess the fall really did mess with your brain. Get a clue, whatever your name is."

"I said it was Adam."

"Yeah, sure, whatever."

"Seriously, though, I have a plan."

"What, we storm his ship with guns a-blazing and

steal back the ten mill? Well, look. No guns. And there's only about one and a half of us, no offense."

"None taken, but I'm getting better. It won't be long now."

She frowned but didn't pursue the subject.

"Okay, I'm game. We got nothing else to do for the next couple of hours. Let's hear it. What's this plan of yours?"

"We slip out of the spaceport, and we let Mada see us."

"It won't matter. My ship is a lot faster than his. I made it special like that. It helps me get out of tight spots."

"Does he know that?"

"He doesn't know about the ship. A girl has to keep her secrets." She smiled coyishly.

"That's fine, but we need him to chase us … and then catch us."

She stopped and turned to Adam, laughing. "You are crazy, aren't you? He'd blast me out of space the first chance he gets."

Adam shook his head while stretching out a grin. "No, he won't. He'll think you have fifteen million credits aboard. That's the last thing he'd do. Let me explain the rest of the plan…"

## 23

Mada Niac was mad as a molting *mulac*. He'd been at the spaceport for an hour, and still no sign of the team he'd sent to the cabin. Could it be possible that Callie defeated them? He gnashed his teeth. He told them to be careful, that they were dealing with a Human. But that also meant that the fifteen million was gone. She would leave with it, and he'd probably never hear from her again. At least, he hoped so. She had a lot of information about him that would prove valuable to certain factions.

He was at his ship with his new crew. He felt awful about his old team; they had been outstanding, almost friends. But Mada Niac didn't have friends. They only got in the way of what had to be done. However, they did have one more task to perform for their fearless leader.

The constable had just arrived. He was delayed by a report of a fire starting in the forest up the mountain. The delay was advantageous, allowing two members of his second team to leave in Cain's ship. It had to appear as if the Human had flown away with the stolen credits. And now, Mada had to put on the performance of his life…

---

After an impassioned and gut-wrenching tale of death and betrayal, the police officer and his team went to the transport and examined the bodies. Then medical personnel tended to Mada's injury, telling him how lucky he was that it was only a grazing wound.

"I pretended to be dead; the Human was out of control. I was fortunate."

"His ship departed an hour ago," the constable reported. "Contact was lost since there was no need to maintain tracking."

"Then he could be anywhere," Mada added.

"Yes. And you report that he took ten million credits from you, part of a negotiation you just conducted?"

"That is correct. I have the contact links for

Bandors Bank on Tactori to confirm. We were to deliver the funds to the bank."

"And where did this negotiation take place?"

"In a cabin about eight miles up the mountain."

The constable checked his notes. "Eight miles and a cabin?"

"That is correct."

"That is the origin point for the fire that is being dealt with at the moment. Could it be related?"

Mada saw his opportunity to embellish the story. "Yes, that is possible so as to destroy evidence. The fugitive we negotiated with is also a Human. I was not aware of that before meeting with her. She had been disguised as a Kalicorean. I believe now that the two Humans were working in tandem."

"Explain?"

"I negotiated a settlement of ten million credits as absolution for her crimes against the bank. She and Adam Cain then planned to steal the ten million back after the warrant was lifted."

"The bank can issue a second warrant."

"Yes, they can, But I was responsible for the delivery of the funds. The fugitives might believe that the terms of the negotiation would remain intact if I did not fulfill my task. Of course, I couldn't because I was supposed to have died with my team. I will contact the bank once we are through and report the theft."

"I will contact them, as well. Is it not odd that a

bank would negotiate with a criminal who stole from them?"

"It happens often; it is what my team and I specialized in." Mada watched as the bodies of his team were removed from the transport and placed on gurneys by the medical staff. He was distraught, almost to the point of collapse.

"I am sorry for your loss, Mada Niac. It was a savage and selfish act. You say the Human's name is Adam Cain?"

"That is correct. And the female Human is Callie Morrison." Mada laughed. "I know; they are strange names."

The constable nodded. "I will check with traffic control to see if they have any trace of the Human's ship. As a recovery agent, I could let you know what I learn. I imagine you may wish to track these criminals yourself. They will be on the Boards momentarily for crimes committed on Kalicor."

"Any assistance you may provide will be greatly appreciated." Then Mada's expression changed from one of remorse to one of pure hatred. "Tactori will also be issuing new warrants. That I can guarantee," he said with venom in his tone. "If I do not find them myself, then others surely will. Justice will be done. It has been my life's work bringing criminals to justice. I only hope it is I who find them."

A few minutes later, Mada was on a link with Champion Tanoric on Tactori. The banker was visibly upset.

"You were responsible for the credits. You know that."

Mada glared at the alien, appearing angry enough to reach through the CW link and grab the banker by the throat. "He killed my team! He almost killed me! And now you say I am responsible?"

"For the credits, not for what happened to your team. Those were the terms of the contract."

"And if I cannot oblige, will you issue a warrant on *me*?"

Tanoric calmed down. "Of course not. All I am saying is that contractually, the credits were turned over to you for return to Tactori. But in light of the tragedy you have suffered, we will amend that portion of the agreement. There will be a warrant issued for the Human, Adam Cain. It will be a large one."

"And what of Callie Morrison?"

"Who is Callie Morrison?"

"That is the true identity of Nija Falonmore. She is a Human, as well. It is my belief that she and Adam Cain are working together. She had no intention of allowing the credits to be returned to the bank. With her warrant lifted and her record expunged, she intended to then meet up with Cain, having lost none of the credits she stole from you—and from me. But I discovered the connection between them. She was not counting on that happening."

Tanoric was silent as he considered what Mada had just told him. It took a moment, but soon the banker accepted Mada's version of the truth.

"We cannot issue a new warrant for the original crime until the time periods have expired. But when they do, there will be an issuance. And Mada, this time, there will be no negotiation with either of the Humans. We may lose all the credits, but it is now time to deliver swift and final justice to these criminals. You may accept the contract or not. But I can see in your countenance that you will be joining the hunt. There will be a reward, but I think that matters not to you at the moment."

"All I want to do is heal up enough so I can form a new team. Cain is not aware that I survived. That will be his downfall. It matters not how long it takes or where the hunt may lead me. And as I take on other assignments and continue to live my life, I will never stop searching for these Humans. They are evil. They must be irradicated."

"I wish to express my condolences on your loss, Mada."

"They were my family, my friends."

"I understand. Now, take care of yourself, and

hurry to join the search. There will be resolution in retribution."

The link was cut, and Mada took a moment to temper his emotions. He had almost convinced himself that he mourned the loss of his team. He did, in a small measure. But the ten million credits in his stateroom made up for it. He silently thanked his former team for their ultimate sacrifice, a sacrifice that was short by two and a half million credits.

Callie Morrison was alive; Adam Cain was not. This Mada knew and no one else. He would do as he said, devote the rest of his life to finding the Human—singular. Unlike the unfortunate Adam Cain, Callie Morrison did do him wrong. And for that, she must pay.

## 24

It was nearing dark by the time Adam and Callie made it into town. The spaceport was still another two miles outside the quaint tourist community of Manisford. The temperature had dropped precipitously, and Adam's shredded clothes weren't doing him any favors. And Callie's clothing was burnt in spots and stained with soot. They were not dressed to impress the snooty inhabitants of the haughty mountain resort town.

"I know someone here," Callie said. "We can find a change of clothing. But she knows me as a Kalicorean, not a Human. I'm missing my elf ears and shoe lifts. It may be an uncomfortable visit."

"A good friend?"

Callie smirked. "Not after tonight."

Adam knew she would do what she had to do.

They weren't able to avoid all the inhabitants, but it ended up not being as big an issue as they thought. A few people came up to them and asked if they could help.

"The fire must have been horrific."

"You are lucky to have gotten out alive."

To the people they met, they were two unfortunate victims of the raging forest fire up the mountain. That worked for the Humans.

The strangers on the street didn't know Callie as a native, so being an alien tourist was fine. They were shown to a boutique store along the scenic, Aspen-like main street and given clothing. All of it had to be rolled up on the sleeves and legs since the natives were taller than Humans, but at least they looked halfway presentable. And since neither of them had any money ("We didn't have time to take our credits before the fire consumed us.") they walked out of the store without spending a dime. And then, no longer standing out like a sore thumb, they hurried to the spaceport and the row of private hangers along the back boundary.

Callie didn't have the key to the lock on the hangar door, but the combined strength of the two Humans was enough to rip the lock to shreds. They kept the large roll-up door closed until they were ready to leave.

Callie's ship was a sweet little custom speedster about forty feet long by twelve wide. It didn't have a lot of creature comforts, with only a single sleeping rack, an efficient built-in kitchen and a head. It did have two seats in front for a pilot and passenger. The passenger seat didn't have any controls like a co-pilot station would have.

What set the ship apart from others were the bulbous twin gravity generators resting along the fuselage and above the two stubby wings. The four focusing rings were in a semi-circle compartment below the cockpit. Four rings and dual generators for a craft this small certainly would give it phenomenal speed, almost racing levels. Adam knew the ship Mada had. It was about six times larger and half as fast. If Callie wanted to run for the stars, she certainly could do it in this ship.

She set about going through the pre-launch routine. There wasn't much to it. The tiny craft also had a set of three rubber tires which allowed it to be driven from the hangar and onto the lifting field. Before leaving the hangar, Adam found a collapsible dolly and put it in the ship. He would need it later.

"I call the ship the *Angel*," Callie said, appearing embarrassed. "What can I say? I like angels. It's registered under the name of Ninja Morrison, a combination of my real and fake names."

"Don't get clearance to lift," Adam said unnecessarily. They'd already discussed the plan.

Callie started the generators to let them warm up and charged the chemical lifting system. Then after they were both strapped in, she engaged the drive motors on the wheels and pulled the tiny craft out of the hangar. Adam found it exhilarating. He hadn't been in something this small in a while. And to pull it out of a garage and then lift off into space was like a kid's fantasy come true. Although he'd been kicking around the galaxy for over thirty years, he still retained that little boy wonder at the reality of space travel. At least the take-offs and landings. He felt the same about air travel back on Earth in the old days. The takeoffs and landings were thrilling. The rest of the trip was boring as hell.

There was plenty of activity in the spaceport that evening, as firefighting ships were taking off and landing constantly. Adam and Callie could clearly see the fire from the spaceport, although it hadn't seemed to have grown much in the last few hours. It would be knocked out by morning, having done minimal damage.

This also presented a problem. The crux of the plan lay in Mada realizing it was Callie's ship leaving the spaceport and then taking flight after it. He would be tied in with the local police by then, being a famous bounty hunter as well as the victim of a heinous crime. But if no one noticed them taking off, then that part of the plan would have to be reworked.

"Don't worry," Callie said. "I got this."

And then she lit off the lifting jets ... and steered

straight for one of the fire control ships that was coming in for a landing. Both ships veered away from each other, missing wingtips by only feet. Immediately, the comm in the small spaceship blew up with complaints from the fire crew, the fire coordinator and the control tower. It seems Callie made an impression.

"Attention, K-143," traffic control yelled. Callie called her ship the *Angel*, but aliens traditionally only used numbers and letters to identify their ships. To traffic control, the ship was the K-143. "You are not cleared to depart. No vector has been assigned. For the dangerous operation of a flying vessel while in an emergency zone, your license is suspended. Return to the field immediately following landing grid Yellow Two. Respond. You are ordered to respond."

Callie didn't respond. Instead, she took a leisurely track into the night sky, giving ground control plenty of time to track her transponder. That would identify her as the owner of the K-143 *Angel*.

"Do we wait in orbit to see if Mada takes the bait?" Callie asked.

"It probably wouldn't hurt, but don't make it look too obvious."

"Okay, here we go."

Callie initiated a shallow gravity-well and shot through the upper atmosphere. Like most worlds in the galaxy these days, Kalicor didn't have an adequate space police force. If a criminal could make it out of the atmosphere, nine times out of ten, they were in the clear. The *Angel* reached orbit, and then Callie began to sputter the generators. It was a clever move. It would make it look as if she was having trouble maintaining a charge. This would work only for a while before the real police showed up. A sitting duck criminal in orbit was an easy target. They would be coming in a few minutes.

## 25

The link came in while Mada was in his ship preparing to leave. He'd brought in the four hired guns he had with him as security for the credits he carried. Between the ambush team on the mountain and these individuals, Mada had already spent some of the credits. He would keep these four with him until he reached Annorac. He had a specialty bank there that held his other funds. They would welcome a deposit of this magnitude and would guard it with their lives. Ten million energy credits were far too much to be carried around with him in the wilds of outer space.

He opened the link with the constable.

"Mada Niac, I have news that may be of importance to you."

"Please speak to me. Does it regard Adam Cain?"

The police official shook his head. "Not of that Human; however, we may have a trace on the other."

Mada perked up. He knew Adam Cain was dead, so that line of inquiry was simply a ruse. But Callie Morrison was another issue.

"Please continue."

"A ship just broke protocol by leaving the spaceport without authorization. It nearly collided with an emergency vessel on the way out. I found the registrant's name to be similar to your missing Human female. It is Ninja Morrison. Does that name have meaning to you?"

*Of course, it does!*

"This could be her," Mada said. "Where is the ship now?"

"We have tracked the transponder into orbit. It is still there, apparently having engine difficulties. I have dispatched a pair of patrol craft to intercept."

"That is excellent news, Constable, yet if I could ask a favor? It would go far to reestablishing my standing with my employer if I were the one to intercept. Considering what a horrible day I have endured, it would be wonderful to have it end on a higher note."

"Of course; I can do that. I will withdraw the patrol craft unless you need them for support."

"I believe I can handle apprehending a solitary fugitive."

The officer laughed. "I imagine you can. Very well,

she is yours to take. Have luck, Mada Niac." He cut the link.

Mada set off in a flurry, barking orders to lock down the ship and prepare for lift-off. Already the generators were running, and the chem jets charged. He just needed to get everyone settled in.

He was in the pilot seat a moment later and made a courtesy call to traffic control. The constable had already informed them of Mada's intentions. He was given immediate clearance.

His ship took off, riding an impressive cloud of grey lifting smoke, which blended with the haze already in the air from the fire in the mountains. The town of Manisford was now draped in the fragrant veil as the night drew deeper and the air more humid. But Mada was soon above it all and racing for outer space. He wasn't sure what he would do once he got there; he couldn't shoot at the ship, not with a potential fifteen million credits aboard. But he *was* experienced in this type of apprehension. Not all his jobs were on planets. Clearly a third of his operations took place in space. His ship was equipped for it.

The constable had relayed the speeder's transponder code to him. Normally, it wouldn't have mattered; since standard private and commercial starships didn't have a way of tracking transponders, only reading them. But he had specialty equipment aboard, the type carried by military vessels. Once locked on, he could follow the ship across the galaxy if need be. And for fifteen million energy credits, he would gladly do so.

The target vessel showed up on his screens, verifying that the energy signal was intermittent. How fortunate—for him—that she had engine trouble only minutes after making her escape. Mada called back to the landing bay. He had magnetic grapples that would work if he got within two thousand feet. That was close, and he had to be careful. Although the vessel was incredibly small, he didn't know what weapons it carried. He gnashed his teeth again in anger, thinking how he knew nothing of this vessel belonging to the Human with whom he'd partnered for almost a year. She kept it from him. But then, perhaps she should have spent more time on maintenance and less time on keeping the ship a secret. That mistake could prove costly.

## 26

"Here he comes," Adam said, reading the energy signals rising from the planet below. He also had the transponder code. He followed the same signal to Manisford when they hopped over from the other side of the planet. "Get ready. Give us some breathing room."

Callie appeared agitated by Adam's side-seat driving. She knew her ship better than he and was probably a much better pilot in it than he would have been. It takes a while to get a feel for a particular starship.

Callie steadied out the generators and kicked the ship into a shallow well, racing off at the fastest acceptable speed near a large gravity mass.

"Keep it at seventy-five percent or below," he advised before he could stop himself. Callie cast him a nasty look. They'd already discussed the strategy, and she didn't need to be reminded. "I'm just saying, sorry."

"Relax, Humie; I won't let him off the hook."

Adam grimaced. Yeah, *Humie* did sound weird. He thought about either Earther or Terran, like from the old sci-fi novels, but no one in the galaxy would know what he was talking about. They rarely did, anyway. He'd just have to convince Callie of his real name sooner or later; maybe use the old line that he was named *after* the famous Human. That worked the best considering his current cloned age. But this wasn't the time for that. His gaze was locked on the signal coming up fast behind them.

"You said Mada caught you before. Did that happen in space?"

"Now that you mention it, it was. But not in this ship."

"So, you've experienced his tactics. Any insights?"

"Good point. His ship was faster than the piece of crap I had then. We exchanged a few cannon blasts—nothing serious—before I gave up. He used magnetics to draw me close."

"He didn't take you inside?"

"My ship was too big. But he does have a cargo bay large enough to hold this ship. He'll bring me inside this time; I'm sure of that."

"Perfect."

Callie was passing the two moons of Kalicor and kicking up the well intensity.

"Set a course for Tactori. Let's give him some incentive to keep coming."

"I think fifteen million credits is incentive enough. But fine; plotting a course for Tactori."

Callie changed course and the trailing signal changed with her. She kicked the well up a little more, a speed that was still exceeded by Mada's ship. She let it sit like this for a while, letting him get ever closer. And that's when she started evasive maneuvers, letting Mada know that her speed was topped out. It wasn't, but he didn't need to know that.

A CW link came through. Callie looked at Adam and shrugged.

"Audio only," he advised.

"Hello, Mada. How's it hanging?"

There was a delay on the link before the alien began speaking. "Let us call a truce," the bounty hunter suggested, cutting to the chase. "We go back to the original terms, twelve million five hundred thousand each. It is only fair. After all, it was you who reneged on our last agreement."

"A little late for that now, isn't it? I'm sure you've already reported to the bank my supposed collusion with the other Human. They will have already issued a new warrant for me. I will be on the run again, and I very much doubt Tanoric will trust me to negotiate a second settlement."

"I have been in contact with Tanoric. A new warrant can't be issued until the time periods expire."

"So, what, six days? It doesn't matter whether there's a warrant now or later. It will only be lifted if you return the money you have to Tactori. I don't suppose that's in your plans, is it?" Callie snorted. "I wonder what Tanoric will say if he learns that it was *you* who broke the contract with him by stealing his money."

"You started it by robbing him in the first place."

"You got that right. It was *my* plan, and it worked perfectly. But now this is about you and me. I would settle for the twelve-five ... if I believed that *you* would really accept that. But after sending your goons to kill me, I'm having a little trouble trusting you."

"Trust goes both ways. Give me my missing two point five million, and I will foul the track following you. I can send the hunters in another direction, perhaps even develop a story that you died, and therefore the warrant is invalid."

"Oh, I'm sure you'll do *that* ... right after you kill me. Instead, why don't you back off and let me go? You have your money, and I have mine. Let's leave it at that. And if you do, I promise not to come after you for trying to kill me at the cabin."

Mada laughed through the speakers. "That is very

generous of you. Of course, that is my major concern at the moment—that *you* would come after *me*. But I must decline your very selfless offer. Instead, power down and allow your ship to be brought aboard. We will work this out in person, as we have done before."

"Again, that's not going to happen. I value life a little too much to do that."

Callie kicked the speeder up another two to three percent in speed, slowly pulling away from the pursuing craft. Mada matched her speed immediately.

"You are at your max capability," Mada said. "Do not waste my time. The outcome is inevitable."

"You may be faster," Callie agreed, "but I can maneuver better."

She cut the link and then went into a stomach-wrenching corkscrew while making a clean forty-five-degree course change to port. Mada was caught off guard and had to double back to get on her tail again. This began a two-hour marathon of course changes and sprints between asteroids within the outer Kalicor system.

Callie frowned. "I wish we could just go in there blasting and take over the damn ship. You know, two Humans could do that without working up a sweat."

"Killing Mada won't serve our purposes."

"Yeah, but we'd have ten million credits."

They'd discussed this already. Adam knew she was only voicing her frustration at having nothing at the end of this. He had already decided to split his share of the recovery fee with her and would have told her then, but he wanted to wait for the right moment. He felt sorry for the ... the thief? That seemed odd.

"Listen," Adam began, "you need the warrant lifted—permanently—and I need to prove I didn't steal the money and kill the bounty hunters. This is the only way."

Callie waved her hand impatiently.

"Yeah, yeah, I know. It's just, well, you know."

Adam patted her on the shoulder. "Keep playing with your pet for a while longer. I'll be in the back making the preparations."

---

Halfway into their planned two-hour game of cat-and-mouse, Adam returned to the bridge and slipped into the passenger seat.

"Are you okay with this?" he asked a frown on his face. It was getting close, and Callie had a major role to play in what was coming.

"Perfectly."

"A lot's riding on you getting back to the *Angel*. Mada is going to have to cooperate for that to happen."

"That's a nice way of putting it. But as I said, don't worry. The great thing about running scams for as long as I have is you learn how to read people, even aliens. The key to a successful con is to anticipate the mark's actions and then use them to your advantage. I'll be ready. And about his ship. It's a Dynon 45a. We learned about those back in Force Recon. I probably know more about the sub-levels than Mada does. And as far as the electronics go, it's simply a matter of switching the leads. A piece of cake."

"Okay then. I have my stuff ready. It won't be big, but it will do the trick."

Callie laughed. "I wish I could be there to see it."

"I hope you aren't. Here, I'll take over for a while; let you go do your magic."

Callie bounded from the pilot seat, and Adam scooted over. She was bubbling over with nervous energy in anticipation of the sting. He felt the same but to a lesser degree. To him, it was more about the launch of the operation, while for Callie was all about the competition. To Adam, most of his operations involved the possibility of death, either his or someone else's. For Callie, a scam was a game, and it was all about winning. But seldom would it involve firearms or the loss of life. Sure, there was the possibility of capture and imprisonment, but she rarely feared for her life while pulling a con.

She went aft while Adam continued with the evasive maneuvers. Two hours should be enough to end of this. He had already decided to split his share of the recovery fee with her and would have told her then, but he wanted to wait for the right moment. He felt sorry for the ... the thief? That seemed odd.

"Listen," Adam began, "you need the warrant lifted—permanently—and I need to prove I didn't steal the money and kill the bounty hunters. This is the only way."

Callie waved her hand impatiently.

"Yeah, yeah, I know. It's just, well, you know."

Adam patted her on the shoulder. "Keep playing with your pet for a while longer. I'll be in the back making the preparations."

---

Halfway into their planned two-hour game of cat-and-mouse, Adam returned to the bridge and slipped into the passenger seat.

"Are you okay with this?" he asked a frown on his face. It was getting close, and Callie had a major role to play in what was coming.

"Perfectly."

"A lot's riding on you getting back to the *Angel*. Mada is going to have to cooperate for that to happen."

"That's a nice way of putting it. But as I said, don't worry. The great thing about running scams for as long as I have is you learn how to read people, even aliens. The key to a successful con is to anticipate the mark's actions and then use them to your advantage. I'll be ready. And about his ship. It's a Dynon 45a. We learned about those back in Force Recon. I probably know more about the sub-levels than Mada does. And as far as the electronics go, it's simply a matter of switching the leads. A piece of cake."

"Okay then. I have my stuff ready. It won't be big, but it will do the trick."

Callie laughed. "I wish I could be there to see it."

"I hope you aren't. Here, I'll take over for a while; let you go do your magic."

Callie bounded from the pilot seat, and Adam scooted over. She was bubbling over with nervous energy in anticipation of the sting. He felt the same but to a lesser degree. To him, it was more about the launch of the operation, while for Callie was all about the competition. To Adam, most of his operations involved the possibility of death, either his or someone else's. For Callie, a scam was a game, and it was all about winning. But seldom would it involve firearms or the loss of life. Sure, there was the possibility of capture and imprisonment, but she rarely feared for her life while pulling a con.

She went aft while Adam continued with the evasive maneuvers. Two hours should be enough to make Mada fuming mad. They needed him to be blinded by his anger.

---

Callie returned a half hour later and handed Adam a small metal box. "It needs to be within two feet. Now, let me take over."

Adam admired her guts. Even though she had worked with him recently, Adam felt he understood how dangerous Mada Niac was better than she. Even after he sent a squad of killers after her, she still didn't fear him. That could prove fatal.

When the time came, Callie made it look as if she'd given up and straightened out the course. She held it steady for fifteen minutes before opening the link again.

"I am growing angrier by the moment!" Mada growled. "Stop this foolish and pointless game. Eventually, your tiny ship will deplete its fuel pod, and long before I deplete mine. And I have extras."

"Then perhaps we *can* renegotiate," Callie said into the comm. She winked at Adam.

"No promises, except to say I will spare your life if you cooperate," Mada said. "Are you now willing to surrender?"

"Surrender is a strong word. Let's just say I agree

to become a guest aboard your luxurious starliner. That sounds a little more inviting."

"Drop out of your well and prepare for grapples. Do it … *now!*"

Mada cut the link.

She leaned back in the pilot seat and looked at Adam. "Okay, we're in. You know he's going to blow his top when he finds out there's no money onboard."

"Hopefully, he'll never find out. I won't need too much time. And I'm trusting that some of your Black Op Force Recon skills come in handy if things go south. None of this matters if we can't get off the ship."

Adam headed aft again.

"See you on the other side, whatever your name is," Callie yelled after him.

"They call me *The Human*," Adam yelled back, a smile in his voice.

"Yeah, that's what they call me, too."

## 27

The *Angel* was slowly brought into the cargo bay of Mada's ship, and once pressure was restored, four armed aliens rushed into the chamber with Xan-fis at the ready. Callie came out of the side hatch. She pulled away the new yellow jacket she got in Manisford to show she had no weapons. The guard searched her anyway, patting her body in inappropriate places. She didn't fret. These were aliens, and so it was like a dog sniffing your crotch; you didn't take it personally. They placed handcuffs on her wrists with the arms in front of her.

Two of the guards led her from the cargo bay while the other two entered the *Angel* to begin the search for the missing fifteen million credits. Callie looked back as she passed through the main airlock, hoping to see

Adam slipping out the back of the ship. She didn't see him.

Callie mentally recorded every step on the way to meet Mada, refreshing her memory from Black Ops training eight years ago. It was something you didn't easily forget. In the past, Callie found herself surveying every vessel she went aboard, looking for access points and weaknesses. It was instinct by now, although she hadn't used any of her training in years.

Mada was waiting for her on the bridge. A Dynon 45a was a fairly large ship, especially considering that it once housed a team of only four bounty hunters. That would make it easier when the time came. The bounty hunter was in the pilot seat with an MK-17 cradled in his lap. He tapped the intensity meter to draw her attention. The weapon was set on Level-1, lethal to a Human. One of the guards remained while the other left, ostensibly to help in the search for the money. So far, Callie had only seen four goons besides the head goon, Mada Niac.

"Callie Morrison," Mada began. "I regret that it has come to this. Our plan was perfect—"

"My plan," she whispered.

"And we were both about to be rich. You ruined it all, and for a minor amount of two-point-five million."

Callie shrugged. "If it was so minor, why did you send your goons to kill me?"

"That was a matter of principle. But now I'm after all of it."

"A needle in a haystack, asshole."

Mada was versed enough with Human-speak to ignore unintelligible words and sentences, finding most to be nothing more than weak attempts at humor. "My crew is now tearing your ship apart."

"They won't find the credits."

"Yes, they will. Even if they have to dismantle the entire vessel, they will."

"I have been doing this for a while. I know how to hide the treasure."

"Fifteen million credit chips? That I doubt. One case of ten million almost broke the back of your former colleague."

Callie frowned. "Have you bought into your own lie? I am not partners with the other Human. Am I to assume he's already met his fate?"

"Yes, the great Adam Cain is dead."

"So … ah, that's what I expected."

Callie had almost blurted out, "So, he *really* is Adam Cain?" but she caught herself at the last moment. She wasn't supposed to know any more about him than the fact that he was to play the part of the patsy., and especially not his name.

"If only I could advertise that fact," Mada continued, "I would become a legend. Many have tried and failed, but it was I who finally killed the famous Adam Cain. It was not that difficult."

In spite of her current predicament, Callie was still overwhelmed by the fact that she was working with *THE* Adam Cain. How was that even possible? He was ancient. But she couldn't give in to the distraction, not now. She had work to do. But if she and Cain lived through this, she would demand a full explanation. He didn't look to be any older than she was, maybe even younger. Was there really a *Fountain of Youth* somewhere in the galaxy, and did he find it? Callie was shocked that she let her mind wander like this. She should be thinking about staying alive.

Instead, she sneezed, lifting her shackled hand to her face and then running her fingers through her flaming red hair and behind her ears.

"I think I'm allergic to aliens."

Mada didn't respond.

After she recovered, she looked back at Mada, locking her eyes with his and holding them. "No matter who he was, Adam Cain served his purpose. Did you accuse him of killing your crew? The cops bought it, I'm sure. But your team must have been shocked when they saw it was you who was going to kill them."

"It did come as a surprise. But as we discussed, they had to be sacrificed. And using Cain to take the blame was a target of opportunity."

"That was a matter of principle. But now I'm after all of it."

"A needle in a haystack, asshole."

Mada was versed enough with Human-speak to ignore unintelligible words and sentences, finding most to be nothing more than weak attempts at humor. "My crew is now tearing your ship apart."

"They won't find the credits."

"Yes, they will. Even if they have to dismantle the entire vessel, they will."

"I have been doing this for a while. I know how to hide the treasure."

"Fifteen million credit chips? That I doubt. One case of ten million almost broke the back of your former colleague."

Callie frowned. "Have you bought into your own lie? I am not partners with the other Human. Am I to assume he's already met his fate?"

"Yes, the great Adam Cain is dead."

"So … ah, that's what I expected."

Callie had almost blurted out, "So, he *really* is Adam Cain?" but she caught herself at the last moment. She wasn't supposed to know any more about him than the fact that he was to play the part of the patsy., and especially not his name.

"If only I could advertise that fact," Mada continued, "I would become a legend. Many have tried and failed, but it was I who finally killed the famous Adam Cain. It was not that difficult."

In spite of her current predicament, Callie was still overwhelmed by the fact that she was working with *THE* Adam Cain. How was that even possible? He was ancient. But she couldn't give in to the distraction, not now. She had work to do. But if she and Cain lived through this, she would demand a full explanation. He didn't look to be any older than she was, maybe even younger. Was there really a *Fountain of Youth* somewhere in the galaxy, and did he find it? Callie was shocked that she let her mind wander like this. She should be thinking about staying alive.

Instead, she sneezed, lifting her shackled hand to her face and then running her fingers through her flaming red hair and behind her ears.

"I think I'm allergic to aliens."

Mada didn't respond.

After she recovered, she looked back at Mada, locking her eyes with his and holding them. "No matter who he was, Adam Cain served his purpose. Did you accuse him of killing your crew? The cops bought it, I'm sure. But your team must have been shocked when they saw it was you who was going to kill them."

"It did come as a surprise. But as we discussed, they had to be sacrificed. And using Cain to take the blame was a target of opportunity."

"He was kinda cute." Callie grinned ... for a second. Then her face turned serious. "But now, how do we resolve *our* differences? Let's face it; if you were in my shoes, you would have done the same thing."

Mada laughed. "If I had the twenty-five million, to begin with, there would have been no deal and no partners. I was pleasantly surprised when you offered to split what you took from the bank with me." Then he shook his head. "None of this would have happened if you had only been honest, telling me you preferred a ten-to-fifteen split. Who knows, I might have even accepted it."

"And your goons would not have come back for the rest?"

"I did not say that. But at the time, you must realize I was upset that you changed the terms of our agreement, and you did it in front of the client. Now I have a problem. Even after I get the credits, what am I to do with *you*? You do like to talk, even if it is Human-speak. Some may eventually figure out that you are telling them *I* was your partner in the theft. They may even believe you."

"They would believe *me*—a thief—over the word of a respected—if quasi—officer of the law? I don't think you have to worry about me telling anyone."

"Not unless you thought it would save you. After the new warrant is issued, you will be hunted again and relentlessly. You will be charged as an accessory in the murders of my team and the theft—for a second time—of the bank's credits. I am sure you would attempt to talk your way out of a situation with the offer of privileged information."

"Again, who would believe me over you? I have no proof. Just let me go, and I promise I'll keep my mouth shut. I might even tell you where the money is."

Mada laughed. "Your ship is tiny. There are only so many places you can hide fifteen million credits. I do not need your cooperation to find it. I needed your cooperation to be brought aboard my vessel and that you have obliged, much to your detriment."

"But you said you would let me live." Callie was near tears.

Mada looked at her, unbelieving. "Do you not know by now that I lie? Much like you, I will say what is necessary at the moment. Most beings do."

Callie pursed her lips. "Unfortunately, if you kill me, you'll never get the fifteen million."

"I thought we just discussed this. Are you saying it is not on your ship? If so, I do not believe you. You would not have left Kalicor without it. When you left, you were not coming back. Am I to assume it was you at your cabin that started the forest fire?"

"Your goons did it while trying to kill me. You should have sent more than eight. I was just warming up when I ran out of goons to kill."

"They were not *Goons*; they were a variety of

species!" Mada shouted in frustration. "There are no *Goons* on my team."

"Fucking aliens," Callie whispered under her breath.

"So, what now?" she asked. The waterworks were really coming down now. She congratulated herself on her stellar performance.

"Nothing," Mada answered. "We wait until your ship has been searched. And if by chance the credits are not onboard, then I will proceed to use more coercive techniques to draw the information from you."

"If I'm to die anyway, why would I tell you?"

"That is easy … so that death will come sooner. You will be begging for me to kill you by the time I grant your wish."

## 28

Adam slipped out the back of the *Angel* just as the two alien goons were entering through the side hatch. He carried with him a backpack with the gear he would need. He crouched along the bulkhead and followed the perimeter of the room around to the airlock exit. It was open, and just as he entered, he heard footsteps on the metal deck coming from inside the heart of the ship.

He ducked back into the cargo bay and squeezed between a pair of fuel tanks as another alien came through the airlock and into the chamber. He went straight for the *Angel* and entered to help the others in the search. The ship was tiny, and three huge aliens bumping into each other would have been hilarious to watch. But Adam had more important things to do.

He passed through the airlock and hurried along

the spine corridor that ran the length of the ship.

Most starships followed the same general design, a long central corridor with pressure doors and joined by numerous connecting passageways to other hallways and compartments. By design, essential components took priority over aesthetics, turning the interior into a maze. Then add to that the fact that Mada's ship had three interior levels, along with a trio of sub-levels, and it was a miracle you could get anywhere without a roadmap. But if the ship followed convention, then cargo, engines, life support and other such departments would be on the O1 level. Living and the mess decks for the crew would be one level up on the O2, and officers, tactical, weapons and the bridge would be on the O3 level.

Mada's ship was far bigger than it needed to be for his original four-person crew. But this was also their home for most of the year—if not full-time. Adam wasn't sure. The fortunate thing for Mada was the ship could be run by a single person, but that wasn't recommended. On the mountain, the bounty hunter had other henchmen, the ones Callie and he killed at the cabin. Then he needed others to steal the *Arieel*. And now Adam knew he had at least four others aboard this ship with him.

Adam knew that Mada thought he was hot shit, so he wouldn't socialize with the hired help if he could avoid it. That meant he would reserve the O3 level for himself. And that is where he would have the ten million credits stashed, probably in his stateroom.

Adam came to a side utility ladder that led up from the O1. It was tight and used mainly for service workers to reach access tubes. He climbed up, passing through a pressure door before reaching the O2 level. He stuck his head into the corridor and listened for signs of life. He had to tune out the constant din of a starship in flight—the creaks, the pops and the hums that were ubiquitous. He didn't hear voices or footsteps on the metal deck. There was a chance all Mada had were the three goons in the *Angel*. He continued up to the O3 level.

Following normal spaceship protocol, the captain would have the cabin closest to the bridge. The corridor jogged here, probably having to conform to a guidance dome or comm relay extending from the hull above. He could hear voices, both Callie's and Mada's. Callie sounded as if she was in distress. He hoped it was part of the act and not the real thing.

Adam raced forward along the corridor, confident that everyone on the O3 level was on the bridge. He had to hurry. The sooner Mada's crew concluded that there were no credits aboard the *Angel*, then things would get dicey for Callie.

There were two doors across from one another at the head of the corridor closest to the bridge. The door on the left was unlocked. Adam slipped inside and looked around. Even though it was an officer's quarters, it was still fairly small. It only took two seconds for Adam to learn that this was not the captain's quarters, and there was no chest of ten million credits resting on the floor.

He carefully opened the door again and moved across the corridor. He tried the handle on the opposite door. It was locked. That was a good sign.

Fortunately, Adam was prepared. It was nothing elaborate, just a pair of long-handled vice grips rummaged from Callie's tool chest aboard the *Angel*. Taking a cloth from the backpack, he wrapped it around the knob to muffle the sound of metal on metal. Next, he clamped the vice grips on the knob and worked the ratchet. Not too tight that he couldn't close the handle and not too loose that the clamping would echo in the hallway.

Just then, Adam heard Callie sneeze. He had to assume it was the second sneeze, meaning he had to hurry.

Adam then twisted the handle of the vice grips, using his Human strength to force the knob to turn. Something snapped, and Adam held his breath, listening toward the bridge for an indicator that the noise was heard. Callie and Mada were still deep in conversation, almost appearing to be having a casual chat about the weather. He was sure it was a little more serious than that.

## 29

Callie wiped her eyes with shackled hands and rubbed her nose. Then she returned her hands to her lap, with the left hand over the right.

"Do aliens sneeze?" she asked. She'd put on a good act of building up to the sneeze, enough so that Mada recoiled, knowing what was coming.

"Of course, we sneeze. Humans are not unique in that regard."

He was growing bored of the conversation and restless for results from Callie's ship. Then he reached forward and opened a comm with the cargo bay. "What is your progress?"

It took a moment for one of the goons to leave her ship and move to a comm station along the bulkhead.

"We are still searching. We are on our second pass but have found nothing."

Mada glared at Callie. Then he said into the comm: "I am coming down. I will find the credits." He looked at her before he left the bridge. "If I do not find them, I will have no patience for any more games. I have ten million credits. If that is all I get, then I will accept that. If so, then you know your fate." Then to the solitary guard. "Watch her … and do not get close. She is a Human. They are deadly." Then Mada left the bridge.

Callie noticed a trace of doubt on the huge alien's face. He had to be seven feet tall, and she barely clocked in at five-three. He couldn't believe this diminutive being could be a threat to him. Good, keep him believing that.

---

Adam slipped inside the room and unhooked the tool before quietly shutting the door. This *was* Mada's stateroom, and there, on the floor next to the bed, was the heavy plastic case that held the ten million energy credits.

Rushing to the crate, Adam flipped back the lid. The backpack slipped off his shoulders, and he withdrew two large cloth bags. In reality, they were pillowcases taken from Callie's sleeping linens. Adam began scooping credits into the bags.

It took longer than he thought, at least until he got to the point where he could pour the remainder into the second bag. Next, he took a metal box out of the pack and placed it at the bottom of the now empty crate. Looking around, he reached over and grabbed a blanket from the bed and stuffed it into the crate, holding the box in place. After this, he set a portable CW comm unit on the box with the screen facing up.

Then came the hairiest part of the operation. He took a one-and-a-half-foot-long metal rod and placed it along the side of the crate until it reached a slot in the bottom box. He carefully lined it up, and once that was done, he brought the lid back into place. Hooking the left side on first, he gingerly placed the top of the rod against the right side of the lid. Taking a deep inhale, Adam pressed down on the lid, hearing a faint click from inside the metal box. And then, applying constant pressure, he snapped the right side of the lid onto the crate.

He held his hands to his side and carefully backed away, not wanting to disturb the crate. It had been a while since he worked with explosives and hair-triggers, but his Underwater Demolition Team training in the SEALS was something one never forgot. The stakes were too high for one not to pay attention during class.

And now, there was no time to linger.

The last thing he removed from the backpack was the collapsible dolly he took from the starship hangar on Kalicor. He'd learned his lesson the first time he hoisted ten million energy credits, almost breaking his back in the process. This time, he would make the job a little easier, if only for as long as he could use the dolly. He tossed the empty backpack under the bed.

With the two bulging bags of credits on the dolly, he moved toward the door, where he immediately ran into a problem. The bags of credits kept melting over the edge of the dolly's platform base and rubbing against the floor. Adam lifted up on the top of the pillowcases but found it was almost impossible to keep the damn bags on the dolly. He should have brought boxes, but it was too late for that now.

He gave up, sliding the dolly under the bed with the backpack before dragging the two pillowcases full of credits over the smooth metal floor. They weren't that hard to move this way, although the plastic chips rubbed against one another, making a hissing sound that stood out from the other noises of the starship. And eventually, he would have to carry the bags down the access ladder.

---

Callie panicked for a second as Mada rushed from the bridge, hoping he wouldn't stop by his stateroom before going to the cargo bay. Instead, he turned right off the bridge, heading for the ladders, and not along the corridor to officer's country. She breathed a sigh of relief.

Then she turned her awareness—if not her attention—to the guard. He was stationed behind her and slightly to her right, across from Mada when the bounty hunter was in the room. With him gone, the grey-skinned creature didn't see a reason to move and remained where he was, leaving Callie's shackled wrists hidden in her lap.

Feeling with her hand for the key she took from under her hair and above her ear with her first sneeze, she quietly worked the pin into the slot and began feeling for the release levels. In her line of work, this was a must-know skill, and within two seconds, the clasp around her right wrist sprung open. These were mechanical locks on the handcuffs. Hidden behind her left ear, she had a tiny electronic key. She came prepared for both eventualities.

Now all she had to do was wait for Adam.

---

Adam moved into the corridor, dragging the bags out with him until he closed the door to the stateroom. He hurried along for about thirty feet before coming to the downward access ladder. Thinking of an easy way to do this, he tied the ends of the pillowcases together, being sure to double the knot against the substantial weight. Then like saddlebags, he hoisted the load over his shoulder. To his surprise, it didn't seem as heavy as before. Perhaps Mada had the gravity set a little lighter aboard his ship than on Kalicor. Or maybe Adam's body was still showing the effects of cloning/healing he was going through after the fall this morning. Either way, this was going to be easier than before.

At the O2 level, he hooked the bags over a bracket on the ladder and then scurried into a side access tube. Built for aliens, Adam had plenty of room in the tube to crawl until he came to a junction box. He didn't know what it controlled; it didn't matter. He removed a small box about the size of a pack of cigarettes from his pocket and set it on top of the junction box. There was a timer on the box. He set it for forty-five seconds.

He scurried back to the access ladder and the bags of money and continued to the O1 level.

There was plenty of activity here, at least from the noise of people talking. He was close to the cargo bay, and he recognized the voice of Mada Niac. He was no longer on the bridge. What did that mean for Callie? Was she with him in the *Angel*, or had he already dealt with her? Surely she would not have gone down without a fight.

With the bags once more draped over his shoulder, he rushed across the corridor and into a side room, confident that all or most of the crew was in the cargo bay or guarding Callie. He hoped they were still guarding Callie.

He looked at his watch. Seven seconds, six…

The explosion could barely be heard, but it was felt throughout the ship. But that wasn't what he wanted. When an alarm began sounding, that was what he was counting on.

People ran past the door to the room where Adam was hiding while Mada barked orders. There were emergency stations every twenty feet along the main corridors, and someone stopped at one and checked the status of the alarm. Adam heard one of Mada's aliens make a report.

"Hull integrity intact. It was an interior explosion. Section J-132, second level."

"That makes no sense," Mada said. Then he yelled for a crewmember to return to the cargo hold while the other two were to accompany him to the bridge.

As they went their separate ways, Adam waited a few seconds to emerge from his hiding place, and then he headed right toward the cargo bay. Through the observation window, Adam saw a lone crewmember near the entrance hatch to the *Angel*. He was armed with an MK-17, which he held casually in his hand. He was looking toward the airlock, waiting for news on what caused the explosion.

Adam grimaced. He had to get through the airlock to reach the ship, and the goon would be a problem.

He reached inside one of the pillowcases and removed a handful of green, twenty-thousand denomination energy credits. Next, Adam crawled across the concourse below the observation window to the inner airlock door and slipped inside. With his back against the inner wall, he tossed the chips into the cargo bay. They scattered past the entrance to the *Angel* and settled on the deck about twenty feet away.

The guard jumped at the tinkling sound of the chips landing and sliding on the deck before being momentarily stunned by what he saw. It was only for a second that he focused on the money from nowhere, which was long enough for Adam to bolt out of the airlock and crash headlong into the taller, bulkier alien.

But Adam had some bulk of his own. Human bone and muscle were denser than that of aliens, which allowed Adam to hit with more force than his size would suggest. He barreled through the guard, knocking him into the hull of the *Angel* and dislodging the MK. Now that the alien was unarmed and it wasn't much of a contest after that. Adam didn't even rush. He allowed the guard to regain his composure and then make a mad rush at Adam, only to be met by a swift uppercut to the jaw. This was Adam's favorite punch since it came from below the taller aliens and could be well hidden.

One punch was all it took, and Adam was soon rushing back to retrieve his pillowcases. But before he reentered the airlock, he went to the cargo bay control station and slipped the small box Callie had given him earlier under the console. And then he raced to the *Angel* with his bags of treasure to wait for Callie … if she was coming.

## 30

They had both felt the explosion if not heard it on the bridge.

The guard stood up straighter and gripped his bolt launcher a little tighter. Callie was sitting in front of him, so he knew she wasn't responsible. Still, he was cautious.

Callie crinkled her nose again and squinted her eyes, raising her hands to her face and preparing for another massive sneeze. To the guard, this was nothing unusual; the Human had done it often. But this time, as Callie fake sneezed, she gripped the stiletto in her right hand and pushed off with her feet on the pilot's console. She slid on the smooth deck on her knees until she was directly in front of the alien guard. She moved unexpectedly and with Human speed. Even more to his surprise, her hands were free.

The stiletto was driven into his gut and left dangling there as Callie rose to her feet. The good thing about having only one cuff of the handcuffs still locked around her wrist was it made for a very lethal weapon, using the free cuff to whip through the air and strike the left side of the alien's face. Already in shock from the knife sticking in his belly, he didn't see the metal ring until it was too late. The sharp, curved edge cut into this skin and nearly took out his right eye. It didn't come out completely but dangled there, held by a thread of tissue and nerves.

With almost a ballerina's balance and flair, Callie spun around, removing the blade from the alien's stomach—and as she completed her pirouette—she planted the tip into the side of the guard's neck. She didn't leave it embedded as she had initially in the belly, thinking she might need the knife later.

Callie was out the door of the bridge a moment later, moving down the main O3 corridor until she came to a grate in the decking. Sliding on her knees to stop her momentum, she grabbed the metal panel and pulled it open. It was an access panel to the O3 sub-level. She flung herself inside, her comparatively small body fitting easily through the opening.

Mada and the two crewmembers reached the bridge only moments after Callie left and found the barely alive guard as he was covered in blood and breathing his last breath. She wasn't on the bridge, so Mada ran out into the corridor. There was no sign of her, and they hadn't passed her on the way to the bridge.

"Back to the cargo bay!" he ordered. "She will be heading for her ship."

No sooner had they arrived at the bridge, the trio was heading back the way they had just come.

---

The sub-level was an access area for energy lines, water, air ducting and other essential components for the ship. Normally, it was termed a *crawl* space. For Callie, it was a *crouch* space.

Her back would regret it later, but she was able to run bent over on two legs before coming to a downward ladder. Relief came to her back as she stretched out, sliding down the ladder by holding onto the side rails with her hands and guiding the drop with her shoes along the outer rail.

And then she was crouching again but making good time. She could still hear the wailing of the alarm set off by Adam's diversion. She knew where she was going and slid down another ladder to reach the O1 level and only twenty feet from the entrance to the cargo bay.

She slowed, careful of any crewmembers who might be present. Callie wasn't sure if Adam was successful with his part of the mission beyond setting off the small bomb on the o2 sub-level.

But then she saw the dead guard outside the *Angel*.

She sprinted through the airlock and into the larger chamber. Adam poked his head up in the cockpit and smiled. Yes, it *is* a nice smile.

She bolted through the open hatch and then stopped to slam it shut and dog it down. She barely got inside her ship before Mada and his two goons raced into the cargo bay, weapons drawn.

One of the crewmembers fired at the hatch. The bolt slashed off the ship, and some of the hot plasma bounced back toward the trio.

"Stop!" Mada yelled at his goon. "MK flash bolts cannot affect the hull of a starship."

Now Mada stepped back and looked to the cockpit. That's when Adam poked his head up again.

The shocked look on the face of the alien was priceless. Adam heard the muffled question through the cockpit glass. "How?"

"I'm a lot harder to kill!" Adam yelled down at him, wearing a huge smile.

Mada shook his head. "I do not know what you

hope to gain. You cannot escape. I can wait you out for as long as it takes."

Callie was at the controls and engaging the drives on the three wheels under the starship. The *Angel* began to turn, the stern moving to point at the huge pressure door at the rear of the cargo bay. She moved the ship forward until the tip contacted the metal of the door.

"You cannot break through!" Mada yelled up to her, having followed along as the ship slowly turned. "I know you have no weapons. You cannot blast your way through."

And that's when Callie sent a tiny burst of lifting propellant into the aft jets. Smoke filled the chamber, and Mada and his people scrambled for the airlock.

"You are insane!" he yelled.

The alien trio went to the control console for the bay. Mada activated a link with the *Angel*.

"Do you propose to send a full charge and force your way through the door? Your fragile ship will not survive."

This link was full audio and video, allowing the gloating Humans to smile back at a visibly angry alien. At that moment, Adam realized he never knew what race Mada was. He'd never bothered to ask. It didn't matter.

"Let's see if what you say is true," Callie chided

while sending another burst through the jets. Adam heard metal crinkle, but not the metal of the door.

Smoke flowed through the interior airlock filling the hallway outside.

Mada began choking until he worked a control on the console and activated the airlock doors, shutting off the cargo bay from the rest of the ship. His eyes grew wide, and his mouth fell open when flashing lights came on, and an alarm began to wail.

The airlock doors *did* close, but at the same time, it activated the atmosphere controls in the cargo bay, and within seconds, the outer door began to open, just the opposite of what was supposed to happen.

Callie waved on the screen. "A little gift from Electronics 101. Just reverse the leads!"

Mada dared not try to stop the process; he couldn't trust the controls not to open the airlock to the rest of the ship and expose them all to the vacuum of space. His lips were like hairlines, and veins pulsed on his thick neck.

"I do not know what you hope to gain," he said. "We have been through this before. I will run you down again."

"Possibly, but at least you don't have my money."

The *Angel* shot out of the bay, riding the reaction force of the now invisible jets. Without air, there was no flame.

"Give me time, and I will," Mada continued on the link. "And I will not be so congenial as I was this time."

Adam sat in the passenger seat, enjoying the banter between Callie and Mada. Then the bounty hunter focused on him.

"I am glad you are alive, Adam Cain. It will now give me more purpose to bring the killer of my team to justice, knowing you will die while resisting arrest."

"Nah, think again, Mada," Callie said. Once again, she reached into her full—and now thoroughly matted—head of long red hair and withdrew a tiny disk-shaped object. "A recorder full of your confession to killing your team. You were also so kind as to speak of stealing the ten million credits and setting Adam up to take the fall. Now, this *is* evidence I didn't have before, and for that, we both thank you. Oh, and by the way, there were no credits onboard my ship. Your stupid goons allowed them to burn up in the fire at the cabin. Oops."

Mada stared into the screen, his thin bottom lip now trembling with anger. "Then you leave me no choice. Rather than hunt you down, I will now blast you to atoms. Your ship is too slow to evade me."

Now Adam grimaced and cocked his head. "And that's where you're wrong, jerkwad," he said. "Just watch."

And that's when Callie engaged a deep gravity-well and sped off to the stars.

Mada wasn't worried; he knew the maximum speed of the vessel. But then he gasped. On the console before him, he blinked at the readings he was getting.

"See, I told you," Cain said. The link was still open.

"Even so, I can still track your transponder. Wherever you go, I will find you. And as Callie so succinctly explained earlier, who is going to believe the word of a thief over mine? Even if you have a recording, it can be faked. That is what I will claim. And now you admit that you have no credits, and all that has happened here has been a ruse. I shall summarize: You have no credits and a fake recording which I will dispute. In the end, you have nothing substantial, while I still have ten million credits."

Cain let out with an offensive sound, something like *Bonk!* "Wrong again, asshole. You're the one who's broke."

And then the Humans cut the link.

Mada fumed. *More of that confounded Human-speak!* What did he mean by the last comment? Mada wasn't injured, so how could he be broke?

But he couldn't dismiss the statement as simply another failed attempt at humor. He sensed it was significant in some way. Curious, Mada softly recited the access code that would activate an alternative context to the statement through the Universal Library. He tensed when the computer voice spoke through his translation bug that the Human word *'broke'* could also refer to wealth, more correctly, the absence of it, as in to have none, to be *broke*.

What could it mean? He was not *'broke.'* He had ten million energy credits—

Mada gasped and then suddenly rushed from the cargo bay, barreling his way past the two confused crewmembers. His stateroom was on the O3 level, and it seemed an eternity for him to reach it. He entered the room, seeing the crate still resting next to the bed. He sat on the side of the cushion and pulled off the lid, hearing a click as he did so.

The chips were gone, all of them! And in their place was a portable CW unit sitting atop a larger metal box. A metal rod lay at an angle along the side of the crate, having just fallen when he lifted the lid.

A commlink was automatically established, and the smiling face of Adam Cain appeared. He rapidly closed one eye and then reopened it.

"Ain't payback a bitch?" was all he had time to say.

## 31

Adam wasn't sure if a ten-second delay would be too long or too short after the lid was removed and the timer tripped. As it turned out, it was perfect. The look on Mada's face was priceless as he realized he was dead, only a split second before the bomb exploded. It wasn't a large bomb, just something Adam threw together out of lifting propellant and some other ingredients Callie had in the tiny engine room of the *Angel*. But it was enough to blow out a nice chunk of Mada's ship and start a chain reaction of cascading explosions. The *Angel* was too far away to witness the final demise of Mada's ship.

Adam shrugged and whispered, "Hasta la vista, baby."

Callie was looking at him, a glow in her eyes he'd not seen before.

"What?"

"Nothing. We'll talk later."

She glanced behind her at the two bulging bags of energy credits.

"To Tactori?" she asked sadness now in her voice.

He nodded. "That's what we agreed on. You're wanted for robbery, but *I'm* wanted for robbery … and murder. It's kind of hard to work in my profession with warrants out for your arrest."

"We don't even know if Mada really reported us. That's a lot of money, and they don't call me *Ninja* for nothing. We could just disappear."

"We?"

"Figuratively, not literally."

Adam shook his head. "Not yet. Let me check with Tidus to see if we're on the Boards."

"Who's Tidus?"

"My boss."

"The famous Adam Cain has a boss?" Callie laughed.

"I sure do, and he's a Juirean to boot." Then Adam caught what she said. "What, now you believe I'm Adam Cain?"

"Mada told me who you are. I don't understand it, but after all of this is over, we have to talk."

"That's fine. But now, I'm calling Tidus."

The Juirean listened in silence as Adam recited the story of what happened over the past five days, ever since he left Tel'oran until he was now in a starship with a foul-mouth Human woman heading for the planet Tactori. They would only continue to the planet if there was a way to get the warrants lifted. If anyone knew if that was possible, it would be Tidus.

"So, you're saying Mada negotiated fifteen percent of ten million?"

Adam was taken aback that out of all he said, the Juirean only focused on the recovery fee.

"That was in the original agreement. Do you think it still applies?"

"Was there a time limit to deliver the funds?"

Adam looked at Callie.

"There was," she said. "It was six days, I think. I wasn't paying that much attention since we weren't going to turn over the money."

"Yeah, I think it was six days," Adam concurred. "Does that matter?"

The pony-tailed Juirean had his computer on. He nodded. "Yes, I see new warrants are on the Boards for both you and Callie Morrison. However, there is a thing called *priority of contract* that might apply."

"What's that?" Callie asked.

"It says that the original contract would take precedence as long as all the terms are met and within the proper timelines."

Adam looked at Callie. "It's been almost two days since the contract was negotiated. Can we get to Tactori in four days?"

She shrugged. "The original six days was based on normal transit time from Kalicor to Tactori. My ship can haul balls faster than that." She pulled up the nav screen at her pilot's station and punched in the numbers. "Damn, it will be close." She looked back at Tidus on the CW screen. "You're saying that if we deliver the money to Bandors headquarters within the timeframe, the warrant will stay lifted."

"For you, it will."

"What about mine?" Adam asked.

"That would depend on whether they accept the recording as proof of innocence. And that would go for Kalicor, too. That's where you supposedly killed the bounty hunters."

"What choice do I have?"

"None, really," Tidus said. "I'll back you up however I can."

"Thanks, buddy. Oh, and one other thing," Adam said to Tidus. "Can you track my ship?"

"You've lost the *Arieel* … again? And as I have said repeatedly, it's not *your* ship. It's mine."

Adam shrugged. "Whatever. But this time, she was stolen by Mada's people. He had to get rid of the *Arieel* to make it look as if I'd taken off with the credits."

Tidus grimaced. "I don't like the sound of that.

That's an expensive ship." He worked his magic on the computer, activating the secret tracking signal Adam had installed in the *Arieel*.

"Good news! It's still active, so they didn't dump the ship into a star somewhere. I'll have the location pinpointed by the time you get done with your business on Tactori. Now, hop to it, son. As I've said before, we need the cash. Things have been pretty lean around here recently."

The link broke.

"I like him," Callie said. "For a Juirean, he's cool."

"I think he secretly wants to be a Human."

"Who doesn't? We're also cool."

## 32

Tactori is a mainline world, rated within the top one hundred in the galaxy, and as such, all rules and regulations were followed to the 't.' Fortunately, all of Callie's licenses and transponders were up to date, and they received clearance to land at the major spaceport outside Randisport, the capital of the planet and the home of Bandors Bank.

Tactori was the financial capital of the old Expansion, and Randisport was a thriving metropolis of over thirty-eight million people, mainly aliens whose financial interests lie in the city. Adam recalled that even Esson Creel had the treasury of Osino deposited in a bank on Tactori. Compared to how much money passed through the planet every day, Callie's theft of twenty-five million wasn't even a rounding error. But it did belong to a bank and its depositors. People tended to take such slights personally.

With ten million credits in cash, it wasn't hard for Adam and Callie to rent a vehicle for the drive into the city. Sophisticated GPS guidance gave them the fastest route to the Bandors Bank headquarters building even though Callie spent almost three months working for the company. The city was so huge that Callie never fully learned it, especially since she wasn't here for sightseeing.

By now, they were counting down the minutes to deadline expiration. The *Angel* did yeoman's work getting them here in only four days. The tiny ship was a bullet, and according to rough estimates, they arrived with two hours to spare.

The credits were now in two boxes and strapped down to a larger dolly from the *Angel*, and after a frustrating drive of an hour and fifteen minutes, the two Humans finally arrived at the towering, two-hundred-story-high building that was Bandors Bank.

They didn't bother parking the transport but instead pulled up in front, unloaded the dolly and then raced inside.

Like any galaxy-wide company, the headquarters building was large, gleaming and meant to impress. The Humans pulled the dolly up to an information kiosk.

"We're here to see Champion Tanoric," Callie huffed.

The yellow-skinned receptionist smiled. "Of course. Do you have an appointment?"

"No, but he will want to see us."

The male creature grimaced and shook his head. "I regret, but no access to one-ninety-four without an appointment. I can connect you to the appointment secretary if you will just take a seat to the right."

Adam stepped up to the counter. He'd healed miraculously over the past four days and showed no sign of his prior injuries. "All you need to do is mention our names: Adam Cain and Callie Morrison. We're Humans. You do that, and Champion Tanoric will reward you handsomely."

"I am much sorry, but you must make an appointment. The Champion leads Bandors Bank. He is very busy."

Adam stepped over to one of the boxes and removed the lid. The shiny green chips were stacked to the brim.

"This is ten million energy credits. They belong to the bank. Tanoric is expecting them in only a few minutes. If you don't call him, we'll leave and take the credits with us. When he learns that we were here and you let us leave … well, let's just say you'll be looking for a new job, if not facing criminal charges."

The greeter stared opened mouthed at the credits.

Although he worked for one of the largest banks in the galaxy, it was a good bet he'd never seen that many credits in person.

"I … I will make an inquiry," he muttered. "But I make no promises that you will be granted access."

"Just make the call. Remember, Adam Cain and Callie Morrison."

The alien made the call, and after butchering their names the first time and needing Adam to correct him, he finally got the message through. He turned back to the Humans with a worried look.

"There are many layers of personnel before reaching the Champion. This could take a while."

Adam looked at his watch. They didn't have a while.

But they didn't need it, either.

Within minutes, alarms wailed, and armed security guards dressed in maroon uniforms swarmed around the pair of unarmed Humans. Adam and Callie raised their hands. This was one of the scenarios they imagined. Not the worst, but right up there with them being shot on sight.

The credits were hauled away, and the Humans were frisked, handcuffed and then led to an elevator. The guards were serious and professional, never taking their eyes off the fugitives during the long ride to the top of the skyscraper.

Another team of security personnel met them at

the top and frisked them a second time while checking their bindings. Eventually, they were led to a conference room that was every bit as large as two *Angels* put together. Six assorted aliens were there already, including one with purple skin and four arms. Adam recognized him as Champion Tanoric. Adam concluded that the title *Champion* was like that of Chief Executive Officer on Earth.

Tanoric was shorter than most aliens but was still around six feet tall. He waddled over to Callie and stared down at her with blazing green eyes.

"You are Nija Falonmore, also known as Callie Morrison. You absconded with company funds." He looked at Adam. "And then *you* stole them again while committing the heinous act of murder. And now you arrive here. What do you hope to achieve?"

"If I may?" Callie slowly reached into the pocket of her yellow jacket and removed the tiny recording disk. "On this recording, you will hear the voice of Mada Niac confessing to stealing the ten million energy credits, as well as the murder of his bounty hunting teammates. He also confesses to making it look as if Adam Cain was guilty of both the theft and the killings when it was he who did it."

Tanoric looked at the disk but didn't take it. Then his gaze locked on Adam.

"You are the one known as *The Human*, a security expert of some reputation. When first hearing that you were joining the team of Mada Niac, we rejoiced. That meant possibly a speedier recovery of our funds. And now you say this recording exonerates you from the crimes you are accused of?"

"Just listen to it," Adam said. "That's exactly what it says. And now we've fulfilled the terms of the original contract. We've delivered the agreed-upon ten million credits and within the deadline." *He hoped.* He'd lost track of time.

Tanoric looked again at the disk Callie still held in her hand. Then he looked to another alien among the crowd. He nodded.

"It seems you have arrived prior to deadline expiration, but barely." He nodded to another alien who came forward and took the disk from Callie. "We will count the funds for accuracy and review the recording. You are to remain here under guard. Authorities have been summoned. Your ultimate disposition is still to be determined."

Tanoric and the other bank officers left the room, leaving only the Humans and the guards. Adam and Callie took seats at the forty-foot-long conference table. They had no idea how long this was going to take. And if it ended with the two of them in prison, it could take a lifetime.

## 33

Four hours later—yes, four long, exhausting hours later—Tanoric and his cohorts came back into the room, but this time accompanied by a pair of aliens wearing matching uniforms but unlike those worn by bank security. They would be the local cops. Were they here to take the Humans into custody?

Adam and Callie had stood up when Tanoric entered the room. He now waved for them to sit back down.

"Upon review and voice identification, we have concluded that it was Mada Niac who killed his fellow recovery agents; however, he cannot be charged with stealing the negotiated funds since he was the one tasked with delivering them to the bank. However, we have released Adam Cain from any such guilt, both for the theft and the murders. We find the crime to be heinous and unforgivable. We have informed Kalicor of these facts, and they will be rescinding the warrant for Adam Cain regarding the murders and the theft and reissuing it in the name of Mada Niac."

Adam breathed a sigh of relief. Good, that was over.

Then Tanoric turned his attention to Callie.

"In the matter of Callie Morrison." His eyes burned with hatred. "We have never before met a subject of a fugitive negotiation in person, and it sickens me to do so. However, with regards to the original contract, the agreed-upon funds were received within the specified timeframe, if not by the designated individual. We shall never condone such an act against the bank and our depositors; however, we are governed by the terms of the contract. The original warrant remains lifted. With regard to the new warrant, that of collusion to steal the ten million credits from Mada Niac, that too will be lifted."

Callie and Adam slapped hands and hugged, causing the alien to recoil from the blatant and violent show of emotion. They settled down after a moment and fought hard to keep from smiling. That might be seen as a death challenge, even here in the rarified air of a bank's conference room.

Now, Tanoric frowned and looked at Adam.

"As per the negotiated terms—those negotiated by

Mada Niac. His team was to receive a twenty percent recovery fee for retrieving the funds. Seeing that you were at one time a member of Mada's team—and the only one now not facing charges—the recovery fee has been assigned to you exclusively and with all subsequent legal implications."

Adam and Callie once again rejoiced. He'd told her he was going to split his thirty percent with her. It wasn't much, about two hundred fifty thousand. But it was better than nothing. It would get her going onto her next scam ... if she decided to stay in the business.

"However," Tanoric continued to say. "Upon an audited count of the funds, we have found that the amount recovered is only eight million, three hundred ninety-nine thousand, nine hundred fifty-two credits, leaving a deficit of one million, six hundred thousand, forty-eight energy credits."

Adam was stunned. So was Callie. They had been figuring on a little shortage. After all, Adam did throw a handful of credits into the cargo bay to distract the guard, and they did take a little for expenses at the spaceport. But over one point six million? Was that what Mada used to pay his goons? Adam shook his head in frustration. That was it, he was sure. Oh well. Fifteen percent of eight million plus was still a lot of money.

But Tanoric was still talking. "Therefore, the deficit has been deducted from the agreed upon recovery fee of one million, five hundred thousand, leaving a balance due Bandors Bank of one hundred thousand, forty-eight energy credits."

Adam was again stunned, but this time almost to the point of tears. So was Callie.

"Wait, you mean we get nothing?" Adam stammered.

Tanoric cast a venomous glare at Callie. "There still remains fifteen million stolen credits. Perhaps Callie Morrison will see fit to share some of her illicit gains with you, Adam Cain. In the meantime, in consideration of the effort you took to return the funds, Bandors Bank had agreed to accept payment of the deficit of one hundred thousand forty-eight energy credits in an installment plan with reasonable interest attached."

Tanoric stood. "I believe this concludes our business. The installment plan will be posted to the Library momentarily with instructions on how and when to pay." He looked again at Callie. "And now, to repeat the words of the thief as she once recited them to me, 'It has been a pleasure doing business with you.' Now, please leave my bank."

---

Adam and Callie stood outside the front entrance to Bandors Bank in shock and drained by what had just happened. Callie was walking away with nothing, while Adam was walking away with nothing, too—plus a bill for over a hundred thousand credits. And for icing on the cake, their rented car had been towed away.

All they had left was the change from the single twenty-thousand denomination credits they'd each taken from the boxes before leaving the *Angel*. Adam had expected to take a little hit on the recovery fee, but to end up *owing* money at the end came as a complete shock to his system.

Then his stomach twisted into knots when another thought occurred to him. *Tidus is going to kill me!*

## 34

Adam had Callie call Tidus to tell him they were leaving Tactori and heading to Tel'o-ran. Adam was in the shower, she said, even though the *Angel* didn't have a shower. But Tidus didn't know that. The last person Adam wanted to talk to at the moment was Tidus Na Nolan. But Adam needed to know where his ship was.

Tidus gleefully gave Callie the information, and then she quickly got off the link.

"He's going to find out sooner or later," Callie said.

Adam nodded. "Let's make it later, okay? A frothing mad, seven-foot-tall Juirean is not a pleasant sight. And I'd rather have my ship back when that happens just in case I have to make a quick getaway."

"He said it was *his* ship," Callie recalled.

"Technically, it belongs to the company."

"Damn," was all she said.

The *Arieel* was on a planet two hundred light-years from Tactori, a place called Vosrum. Adam had heard of it but had never been there. Callie agreed to take him there if he covered the cost of the fuel pod. He had nine thousand credits left out of the twenty thousand he started with after paying the impound fee for the rented transport. That would pay for a cheap recharged fuel pod for the *Angel*.

On the bright side, it was inevitable that through all they'd shared over the past few days, Adam and Callie eventually gave in to their carnal desires and hooked up. It had been a while for both of them. Callie found aliens to be repugnant and never got that desperate. Adam snickered when she told him that, thinking she's never met a Formilian male. That would have changed her mind about alien hook-ups. He didn't tell her about Arieel Bol, his ship's namesake and the mother of his daughter, Lila. Arieel was a Formilian and the only alien he'd ever been with; however, none of the Humans who knew about the relationship ever questioned him for doing so. Arieel was commonly referred to as the Most Beautiful Prime Female in the Galaxy. Who would blame him, right?

So for Adam, it had even been even longer since he'd been with another Human. It felt right, natural.

They first got together on the way to Tactori. But on the trip to Vosrum, the mood and passion were decidedly less robust. Even sex couldn't salve their bruised egos and empty pocketbooks.

Upon landing on the planet, Callie spent half of her remaining money on a pair of used MK-17 flash weapons. Adam figured he'd need one to get his ship back. Callie got hers in case he needed backup. But by now, she knew Adam could take care of himself.

On the four-day trip to Tactori, Adam ended up telling her his life story, a story which left her speechless and stunned. It sounded like something out of a cheap science fiction novel about alien empires, inter-dimensional travel and immortal mutants who could clone human beings. But here he was, living proof that cloning was possible. She knew for a fact that Adam Cain had to be in his late fifties. Yet the twenty-something-year-old body he now inhabited was living proof of at least part of what he told her. She would reserve judgment on the rest of the tale until she'd had a chance to read *The Human Chronicles Saga* for herself.

Still, she was amazed and impressed by how Adam seemed to take most things in stride. He'd seen and done more than any other Human in history, and yet he was still down to earth and relatable. *Damn, the dude actually died!* And here he was back for a second round of living. She admired his tenacity, and it helped put all her personal trials and tribulations in perspective.

It also scared her. She really liked the guy, but who could think of a future with a personality as large as

Adam Cain? In one respect, he was kind and approachable. In another, he was larger than life, a hero, a legend. It was intimidating as hell.

And that's why she decided to leave as soon as she helped him get his ship back. Adam Cain tended to dominate all the air in a room. That's what people often said about her. Her ego was too big to let it be dominated by someone else.

---

Adam had the coordinates for the *Arieel* programmed into his datapad, and for a few leftover credits, he and Callie rented an ancient transport and headed into the seedier part of an already seedy town looking for the address.

Alien worlds came in all varieties, and Vosrum was what one would call a melting pot. It once served as a major stopping point for long-haul spacers needing fuel pods, but like a town passed over by the rail line or major freeway on Earth, it was soon forgotten and neglected. Now it served as a no-holes-barred center for hundreds of gangs and minor cartels, a place where they could resupply and regroup, preparing for their next illicit foray into the galaxy.

The transport barely crept along at twenty miles per hour, its overused batteries barely able to hold a charge these days. Callie was worried about the *Angel* back at the spaceport, and Adam offered to drive her back. He could get the *Arieel* on his own. But she said no; he might still need her help.

The neighborhood was dark, wet and dreary, made up of dozens of ancient warehouses, most with their large rollaway doors gone and housing hundreds of homeless creatures of an unimaginable number of species. What they lived on and ate was anyone's guess, but Adam figured most saw their neighboring aliens as more of a food source rather than a fellow compatriot sharing in common despair.

What the *Arieel* was doing in a place like this was also a guess. It was an expensive and sophisticated vessel which meant it would bring a pretty penny, here or on a hundred nearby worlds, either in whole or in parts.

The closer he got to the address, the more depressed he became. The *Arieel* was his home, and everything he owned was aboard. He firmed his resolve that if he got her back this time, he would put more of his most-precious memorabilia in a storage locker on Tel'oran, someplace safe and not subject to the vagaries of his job. Adam lived a dangerous life, and he was forever placing his ship in jeopardy. That wouldn't end. But he hated having his shit rummaged through and stolen. Hell, he was surprised he still had anything left by now.

There was a lot of activity at the address. It was a

cluster of three warehouses, with the doors still intact but open and a couple of dozen grimy aliens working welders and cutting torches, the dancing sparks almost the only light in the buildings.

It was an alien chop shop, and the bastards had the *Arieel* here for over a week. It would be a miracle if anything was left.

Adam pulled up to the main building, checked the charge on the MK-17, and then bounced from the car. He didn't wait for Callie. He was singularly focused on finding his ship.

No one stopped what they were doing as Adam stormed into the cavernous structure. It could hold a half dozen *Arieels*, and it looked as if it did. There were skeletons of starships, ground transports, and even cold fusion reactors, all being broken down into their most elemental parts. This was a big operation on a little world and probably run by one of the major Cartels like the Gradis or the Hanroc Brigade.

And then he saw her. The *Arieel* was in the back, outside on a large field, sitting in a queue for her turn at the cutting torch. Adam worked his way through the clutter and flying sparks to reach the ship; his heart was overjoyed that the hull appeared intact.

Adam gripped the MK tightly in his right hand—they couldn't afford holsters or even extra batteries for the weapons. He had the gun set on stun, not because he was feeling magnanimous, but because he needed as many debilitating shots as he could get out of a single charge. No one was around, so he went inside the open hatch.

Again, much to his relief, all the components were still in place. Sure, his stuff was strewn around the interior, but it seemed to all be here … for now. He knew that if left up to the chop shop, all his stuff would either be tossed in a dumpster or sold to the street merchants as a single lot. The real money was in the *Arieel* herself. Perhaps the reason she was still in one piece was that the gangsters were trying to offload her in a single transaction, even if the parts could bring more money.

"No attendance!" a gravelly voice called out to him as Adam came out of the hatch. Callie had her eyes locked on the alien as he strode up to the Human.

He was tall—as usual—and looked like Arnold Schwarzenegger in his prime but covered in grease and grime that seemed baked into his scaly skin.

"Leave, now. You no be here."

"This is *my* ship," Adam barked at the alien. "I'm taking her back."

This stopped the huge creature in his tracks. Black, glassy eyes bore into Adam even as a sinister grin stretched across his cracked lips. "No, your ship … no more. I bought. Will sell back."

"Bullshit," Adam replied. "I'm not going to pay a

cent. It was stolen from me, and I'm reclaiming my property."

Five more of the chop shop workers had gathered around. None appeared armed, except with heavy metal tools they held in their blackened hands. Callie moved in closer to Adam, who stood outside the airlock hatch to the *Arieel*. If anything, the ship would provide some cover should it become necessary.

Arnold the Alien looked over the pair of Humans and nodded. "You have credits; I tell from clothes." He had a point, Adam thought. They were still wearing the free clothing they got at the boutique on Kalicor. They weren't cheap … if they had to pay for them.

"Look, I'm not leaving here without my ship. This can go easy, or it could go hard. You do realize what we are, don't you? We're Humans. Just think about that before you do something stupid."

"Humies?" Arnold exclaimed. "They bigger. You not. Not big or Humies."

Adam grimaced. He really didn't like the label *Humie*. He'd never heard the term before Callie mentioned it. And now Arnold was using it. Adam pointed the MK at the alien leader.

Arnold looked at it and laughed. "Even if you get ship, how you get it from here? Ship towed. You have no tow."

"Let me worry about that," Adam said. And

worried he was. There was only one way out of here, and that was straight up.

"No. You worry bout life. Take him!"

Adam opened up with the MK, followed a split second later by Callie. Most of the smaller aliens succumbed to the stun bolts but not hulking Arnold. He grimaced and groaned, but he didn't go down. Instead, he stepped forward and slapped the weapon from Adam's hand while reaching out with a twenty-inch-diameter hand, one large enough to encompass Adam's entire head. The beast lifted him off the ground and threw him against the hull of the *Arieel*.

Callie had her own problems and couldn't help. She had rapidly depleted the twenty stun bolts she had in her MK and now had a three-foot-long wrench in her hands that she'd taken from one of the fallen and was swinging it wildly out in front of her to ward off even more attackers from the chop shop. They were all in the game now, preferring a quick fight with a couple of Hobbits to their more mundane cutting and welding chores.

Adam was on his own, pressed against the hull with his feet dangling two feet off the ground. His arms were free, and rather than use his hands to force the alien's hand off his head, he used them to pummel Arnold with a dozen quick blows to the creature's face. The beast seemed to be made of stone, but eventually, he got the message. He used his free hand to strike back but found it hard to make it past Adam's swinging fists. Eventually, he grew weary of Adam's constant hits that he tossed the Human aside like a bag of trash. Adam landed hard on the ground and then watched as Arnold looked around the field for a weapon. He found one: a four-foot-long metal pipe, one of the hundreds that lay scattered on the dirt.

"Get inside!" Adam yelled to Callie. She was already working her way there, keeping a horde of angry aliens at bay.

"I can help," she yelled out.

"No, save yourself. I can take care of this one."

She ducked inside the ship and slammed the button to close and lock the hatch.

With their target gone, the other aliens turned their attention to Adam.

"No! Mine!" Arnold yelled.

Adam breathed a sigh of relief. One Alien Arnold he could handle. But not Arnold and his twenty minions.

Adam wasn't injured, yet he was unarmed, and Arnold was moving toward him, swinging the metal rod to and fro while flexing his pectoral muscles and beating on them like bongo drums. His teeth were fully exposed in what was the true meaning of an alien death challenge.

"Listen, is the ship really worth losing your life

over?" Adam asked as he deftly stepped back, staying out of range of the metal bar.

"Is for you, too?"

Adam smirked. He had a point.

Adam continued to move along the hull, slipping around the back of the ship with Arnold slowly stalking him. The alien was in no hurry, and as more of the workers gathered around to watch the show, he seemed to revel in the attention. It was always good now and then to demonstrate his physical superiority. It helped maintain his control over the hired help.

That's when Adam heard the generators spin up aboard the *Arieel*. Callie was at the controls and revving up the engines. The chem jets were also being pressurized. The problem: Adam was outside the ship, and the airlock door was locked.

Adam continued to evade the huge alien as he slid along the port side of the ship and closer to the cockpit. He glanced up and saw Callie looking at him from above. She yelled something, but he couldn't make it out over the roar of the alien crowd as they chanted for Arnold to smash him to bits. Finally, Callie lifted her hands into the air while mouthing something like looked like *jump*.

And so he did. Using his Human muscles in the light gravity of Vosrum, he bounded up maybe fifteen feet. It wasn't enough for him to reach the top of the cockpit, but it was enough for him to grab hold of a comm antenna jutting out from the side of the ship.

Adam pulled his legs up just in time to avoid a clanging blow of the metal rod from Arnold. It rang against the hull, sounding like a gunshot. With the alien's height, arm length and four-foot-long rod, he could easily reach twenty feet up, and so he swung again, requiring Adam to swing on the antenna back the other way to avoid getting hit. Arnold let out a screeching cry of frustration that was cut short by an incredible blast of lifting gas as Callie engaged the chem jets.

The field was now completely obscured by the cloud of smoke, and the force of the blast shot through the warehouses, blowing out the walls on the other side. Bodies were tossed about as if caught in a tornado.

Adam continued to dangle from the thin antenna, thinking that at any moment, it could break. Callie kept looking out at him, worry creasing her forehead.

"Hold on!" she yelled, although Adam could only read her lips over the roar of the lifting jets.

Glancing down, Adam saw the whole of the chop shop was in ruins, with gas clouds billowing along the side roads as aliens panicked and ran. That'll teach them, Adam thought. Steal my ship, will you … even though technically it belonged to Tidus.

Callie had no idea where she was going, but she

went slowly, giving Adam time to firm his grip on the antenna. There was a topside access hatch on the *Arieel*, but at the moment, there was no way for Adam to get there. She would have to land somewhere, anywhere.

This part of the town was nothing but miles of ghetto clusters with not an open space in sight. Adam had his arms locked on the antenna, and as long as it didn't break, he was fine. Callie kicked the accelerator up a little and headed for the outskirts of the city and the spaceport. As the crow flies, it wasn't too far. She kept glancing out at Adam to make sure he was okay. He gave her a thumbs up, although his teeth chattered from the cold.

Although the frigid air sweeping over his body was excruciating, he felt warm inside. He was clinging to the side of his beloved *Arieel*. All was right in the world, that was until he got back to Tel'oran.

---

Callie set the *Arieel* down not far from the *Angel*, ignoring the cries from traffic control that she had no right to be in their airspace. The moment she touched down, Adam let go of the antenna and collapsed on the ground, coughing and choking from the second round of jet exhaust. Recovering, he dashed off to clear air about a hundred yards away.

After the gas cleared, Adam was at the hatch as Callie met him there with a giant bear hug.

"You really do need to keep your ship from being taken," she laughed in his ear.

"I'm trying," he laughed back. "Now grab the *Angel*, and let's get the hell out of here."

"Right behind you, Captain Cain, sir."

---

They cleared Vosrum airspace fifteen minutes later and then separated the ships so they could engage dual gravity-wells. Adam set a course for Tel'oran, and that's when he noticed something strange on the nav screen.

"Where are you going?" he asked. "Tel'oran is this way."

"I know, sweetheart, but I can't come with you."

"Why not?" Adam asked, stunned.

"I helped you prove your innocence, and now you have your ship back. But I can't go any further."

"I thought we—"

"I know what you're going to say. But we're two of the same personality types. It wouldn't last, and you know it. I'm just thankful that I got to experience the legend of Adam Cain in person. I never dreamed that would happen."

"C'mon, don't be like that. I'm not a legend; I'm just a person, just like you."

"Yeah, keep telling yourself that."

There was silence on the link as Adam couldn't think of anything else to say. He looked into her blue eyes and at her flaming red hair and thought of what might have been. But she was right. This was the reason Adam wasn't back on Earth. Celebrity was not all it was cracked up to be. Living his life as the anonymous *Human* was preferred to always being measured against past deeds and past glory. Still, it was a lonely existence.

"All right, I understand," Adam said finally. Then he smiled. "Hey, it was fun while it lasted."

Callie frowned. "Fun? Are you fucking kidding me? My latest caper ended in disaster, and now I'm broke and with barely enough fuel to get me back to my base planet."

"It doesn't have to be like that. You could come back to Tel'oran with me—"

"And watch you get fired by your green-skinned Juirean boss? No, thank you. You have enough worries of your own to deal with. You don't need me hanging around."

"What are you going to do?" Adam asked.

Callie smiled wickedly and winked.

"Anything I can get away with."

## EPILOGUE

*Yeah, this isn't going to be pretty,* Adam thought as he set the *Arieel* down in the executive spaceport outside Dal Innis on the planet Tel'oran. He still hadn't told Tidus about the loss of the recovery fee and how Adam actually ended up *owing* money after his latest assignment. That was a first. But he knew Tidus was only being melodramatic about the company needing the money. They were doing fine. Or at least Tidus's other agents were doing fine. And Adam did have a sizeable backlog of commissions due. Not a hundred thousand credits worth, but it would be enough to get back on his feet. It just meant he'd have to work a little harder to get square with Tidus. The Juirean wasn't only his boss but also his friend. They'd been on many an adventure together, and it would take more than a couple of lost fees to spoil that. Wouldn't it? He hoped so.

Still, he was reluctant to face the Juirean.

---

Adam was in his stateroom, trying to decide what to wear to his funeral, when he heard banging on the airlock hatch. His spaceship didn't have a doorbell. He also didn't get a lot of uninvited visitors.

Maybe it was Tidus. *Oh shit,* Adam thought. He was so anxious to get the one point five million credit recovery fee that he came out to the spaceport himself to get it.

*Oh well,* Adam thought. *It was going to happen sooner or later. Might as well get it over with.*

Adam moved to the airlock and activated the hatch.

To his shock and utter amazement, it wasn't Tidus.

---

"Well, fuck me! I had to see it to believe it. Excuse me, son, but is your *dad* home?"

The smile on the big man's face was intoxicating and both a relief—that it wasn't Tidus at the door—and also a shock for who it was.

"General Todd Oakes, what the hell…?" Adam said.

The big man stepped in and shook Adam's hand before pulling him in for a powerful man hug. "I heard about what happened to you, but you know, who can believe the stories? Is it really you? Well, thank god for immortal mutant geniuses. They really did a number on you, didn't they?"

"What are you doing here, General?"

"I came looking for you. Can we come in?"

"We?"

"Yeah, I brought a couple of scoundrels with me. Part of the old Navarus crowd."

He leaned out of the hatch and waved his hand.

A moment later, Mike Hannon and Jay Williford were in the airlock, hugging and slapping Adam on the back.

"Why are you here? Did I miss a class reunion or something?"

Adam didn't know how to take the surprise visit from some of his oldest friends and acquaintances. It had been years, and even though they were a distraction from his worries with Tidus, he couldn't help but suspect something strange was in the air.

Here was General Todd Oakes, former commander of the Human garrison on Adam's second homeworld of Navarus, which, for Adam, was literally another lifetime ago. Also, Mike Hannon, a skilled—

yet hopefully reformed—alien assassin, along with the not-so-young-anymore Jay Williford, one of Adam's old Enforcers from the time when he ran the police force for the Dead Zone. Adam wasn't even aware they knew each other that well. The only common denominator they had was him, the original Adam Cain.

He invited them in and provided drinks from the processor, after which there was about a half hour of casual banter and catching up before Adam grew impatient and cut to the chase.

"All right, guys, what's this really all about? You didn't just happen to all be on Tel'oran and knocking on my door. I just got back today. You've been waiting for me."

The General naturally took the lead; he was used to being in charge.

"Yeah, you caught us," Oakes said with a smile—a guilty smile. "We came looking for you when we learned that the famous *Human* bounty hunter was none other than our old friend Adam Cain. I wondered why you didn't come back to Earth after the Klin thing dried up. Then I ran into Sherri and Riyad. They told me about the cloning and how you were starting a second life, one where you can fly under the radar and not be hounded by your past." He snorted. "Yeah, how's that working out for you? You can take the kid out of the hero, but you can't take the hero out of the kid. I just made that up."

"Not to be rude, but what do you want?"

Mike Hannon leaned forward on the couch in the *Arieel's* common room. "To be honest, Adam, we need a leader."

"A leader for what?"

"For a little operation we're putting together."

Adam sat back in the chair as alarm bells went off in his head. Mike Hannon's brand of operation usually meant assassinations that nearly set off galactic wars, like when Adam first met him on Navarus. That was a long time ago, and obviously, Mike hadn't changed.

"What kind of operation?"

Mike grinned. "Well, it's kind of a heist."

"A heist, like in stealing stuff?" Adam asked.

"Like in stealing a *lot* of stuff," Mike said cryptically, his eyes alight with larceny.

Adam snickered. Mike Hannon was up to his old tricks again. And Jay Williford was just a step or two behind him as a wannabe conman. But he was surprised to see the General mixed up with these two —what was the word Oakes used for them—*scoundrels*. Hell, Adam just got out from under the cloud of a *heist*, and he wasn't about to jump right back into another. Besides, Tidus was expecting him…

Adam mentally shrugged. Tidus … or a few more minutes with his friends? Oh well, they'd come this far. He might as well hear them out. "Okay, go ahead. Tell me about it."

It was Jay's turn to fill in the blanks.

"It's a depository, a type of bank. We think there could be as much as half a billion energy credits in it."

Adam laughed and looked at Mike. "Did you put them up to this? It sounds like something you'd do. Getting kind of ambitious, aren't you, buddy? Robbing a bank and for half a billion credits."

Hannon wasn't put off by Adam's negativity. Instead, the smile remained.

"Just hear him out," Mike said, and Jay continued.

"It started with the General. He'd been tracking the settlements; there are six of them, you know. They've been collecting credits for the other colonies. It's all there, just ready for the taking."

"What, what are you talking about?" Adam asked, confused. "What colonies? And what makes you think you guys could get away with stealing half a billion credits? You're not crooks, at least not all of you." He looked again at Mike. "Where exactly is this bank of yours?"

"It's in the Devil's Gate…." General Oaks said, letting his voice trail off.

The words hit Adam like a brick to the face. He fell back in his chair. "Devil's Gate? You mean like in the *Klin* colony at Devil's Gate?"

"That's right," Mike said. "One of the six colonies the Klin established after their failed invasion of the galaxy."

"After the loss, they split their remaining forces into six," Oakes said, taking over the narrative. "They didn't want to consolidate all their population in one place to give us a unified target. They just wanted to slip away somewhere where they wouldn't be a threat. The allies accepted that since we were in no shape to launch an offensive against them at that time. Now, it's kind of a live and let live arrangement."

"Anyway," Mike said impatiently. "The Klin have a bank in Devil's Gate where they've been collecting their credits. They still need supplies, and they use the money to trade with people outside the Gate. Some of these traders have come back with stories of the wealth the Klin have built up. And you know the Klin. They're one big happy family of silver-skinned bastards, so security at their master bank is virtually non-existent. Hell, it's not like they're going to steal from themselves, right?" Mike grinned broadly. "So, we waltz right in and come out with a king's ransom."

"Stealing from the Klin?" Adam's mind raced with the possibilities. "Okay, fine," he said, "but why me? Why bring me into this?"

"Because you have a knack for surviving weird-ass missions," Oakes said. "And we've been following your career. *The Human* has a reputation for getting things done. And besides, we know you. We've all worked with you in the past, and if anyone can lead such an operation, it's you."

"Hey, you're the General here, not me," Adam countered.

Oakes snickered. "I'm just an aging desk jockey now. What we need is some young blood—with experience. Hell, you're even younger now than Jay, but you have over thirty years of experience under your belt."

Adam shook his head, not from discarding the idea but from habit.

"But to rob a bank and think you can get away with it. Really?"

Mike leaned in again. "Need I remind you? It's ... behind ... enemy ... lines," he said slowly for effect.

Adam sat for several seconds, cataloging his thoughts on this matter and others. He was nearly broke; he owed over a hundred thousand credits to a bank on Tactori, and there was a good chance he could get fired from his job with Starfire Security at any moment. And unlike the bank that Callie robbed, this one *was* behind enemy lines....

Adam's eyes lit up, and he grinned, matching the wickedness in Mike's smile.

"This could be the perfect crime," Adam whispered. And then, with enthusiasm ... "Count me in!"

**THE END**

**of**

# Human for Hire (2)
## Soldier of Fortune

and the beginning of
## Human for Hire (3)
## Devil's Gate

# HUMAN FOR HIRE (3) — DEVIL'S GATE

Be sure to sign up for the email list to get updates and notices of the new books coming from T.R. Harris.

# AUTHOR NOTES

Thank you for reading **Human for Hire (2) – Soldier of Fortune**. I hope you enjoyed it.

As you can tell, there is a major backstory involved in *The Human*. This is detailed in the 44 books that make up **The Human Chronicles Saga**, **The Adam Cain Saga** and **The Human Chronicles Legacy Series**. If you want more Adam Cain, I have plenty to offer!

Going forward, after this book, I'm taking a little time off to do some housecleaning. I will be going through ALL of my books, making needed corrections, updating bibliographies, adding the first chapter of the next book in each novel, getting all of the books made into paperback, while at the same time the books are being produced in audiobook form. A lot are already in audio, but soon, they all will be.

This has been long overdue, but when you have 58 books out (plus seven box sets) that's a lot to catch-up on. Eleven years of work that needs to be updated. But in the end, I think it will be worth it. It will provide a better experience for my readers.

About the new **Human for Hire** book.

It's called **Human for Hire (3) – Devil's Gate** and is fashioned after the old Clint Eastwood movie **Kelly's Heroes**. I've always enjoyed that movie and have been wanting to adapt it to science fiction. Here, a team of Humans go after a wealth of Klin credits held in their private enclave within the Devil's Gate region of the galaxy. As with the movie, there's a ton of humor in the story, along with successes and failures. And of course, the requisite twists and turns that I have so much fun springing on my readers. Don't get too comfortable; things could change in an instant. **Gotcha!**

So, short and sweet.

Be looking for **Human for Hire (3) – Devil's Gate** available NOW. Until next time.

**T.R. Harris**

September 2022

## FACEBOOK GROUP

I'm inviting you to join my exclusive, secret, Super Fan Facebook Group appropriately called

***Fans of T.R. Harris and
The Human Chronicles Saga***

Just click on the link below, and you—yes, **YOU**—may become a character in one of my books. You may not last long, and you may end up being the villain, but at least you can point to your name in one of my books – and live forever! Maybe. If I decide to use your name. It's at my discretion.

**trharrisfb.com**

**Contact the Author**

## Facebook
*trharrisfb.com*

## Email
*bytrharris@hotmail.com*

## FACEBOOK GROUP

I'm inviting you to join my exclusive, secret, Super Fan Facebook Group appropriately called

### *Fans of T.R. Harris and The Human Chronicles Saga*

Just click on the link below, and you—yes, **YOU**—may become a character in one of my books. You may not last long, and you may end up being the villain, but at least you can point to your name in one of my books – and live forever! Maybe. If I decide to use your name. It's at my discretion.

**trharrisfb.com**

### Contact the Author

## Facebook
*trharrisfb.com*

## Email
*bytrharris@hotmail.com*

# NOVELS BY T.R. HARRIS

## Technothrillers

*The Methuselah Paradox*
*BuzzKill*

## Human for Hire Series
*Human For Hire*
*Human for Hire 2 – Soldier of Fortune*
*Human for Hire (3) – Devil's Gate*
*Human for Hire (4) – Frontier Justice*
*Human for Hire (5) – Armies of the Sun*
*Human for Hire (6) – Sirius Cargo*
*Human for Hire (7) – Cellblock Orion*
*Human for Hire (8) – Starship Andromeda*
*Human for Hire (9) -- Operation Antares*

*Human for Hire (10) – Stellar Whirlwind*
*Human for Hire (11) -- I Am Entropy*
*Human for Hire (12) – Earth Blood*
*Human for Hire (13) – Capella Prime*

**The Human Chronicles Legacy Series**
*Raiders of the Shadow*
*War of Attrition*
*Secondary Protocol*
*Lifeforce*
*Battle Formation*
*Allied Command*
*The Human Chronicles Legacy Series Box Set*

**The Adam Cain Saga**
*The Dead Worlds*
*Empires*
*Battle Plan*
*Galactic Vortex*
*Dark Energy*
*Universal Law*
*The Formation Code*
*The Quantum Enigma*
*Children of the Aris*
*The Adam Cain Saga Box Set*

**The Human Chronicles Saga**

*The Fringe Worlds*
*Alien Assassin*
*The War of Pawns*
*The Tactics of Revenge*
*The Legend of Earth*
*Cain's Crusaders*
*The Apex Predator*
*A Galaxy to Conquer*
*The Masters of War*
*Prelude to War*
*The Unreachable Stars*
*When Earth Reigned Supreme*
*A Clash of Aliens*
*Battlelines*
*The Copernicus Deception*
*Scorched Earth*
*Alien Games*
*The Cain Legacy*
*The Andromeda Mission*
*Last Species Standing*
*Invasion Force*
*Force of Gravity*
*Mission Critical*
*The Lost Universe*
*The Immortal War*
*Destroyer of Worlds*
*Phantoms*

*Terminus Rising*
*The Last Aris*
**The Human Chronicles Box Set Series**
*Box Set #1 – Books 1-5 in the series*
*Box Set #2 – Books 6-10 in the series*
*Box Set #3 – Books 11-15 in the series*
*Box Set #4 – Books 16-20 in the series*
*Box Set #5—Books 21-25 in the series*
*Box Set #6—Books 26-29 in the series*
**REV Warriors Series**
*REV*
*REV: Renegades*
*REV: Rebirth*
*REV: Revolution*
*REV: Retribution*
*REV: Revelations*
*REV: Resolve*
*REV: Requiem*
*REV: Rebellion*
*REV: Resurrection*

*REV Warriors Box Set – The Complete Series – 10 Books*
**Jason King – Agent to the Stars Series**
*The Unity Stone Affair*
*The Mystery of the Galactic Lights*
*Jason King: Agent to the Stars Box Set*
**The Drone Wars Series**

*BuzzKill*

**In collaboration with Co-Author George Wier...**

**The Liberation Series**

*Captains Malicious*

Milton Keynes UK
Ingram Content Group UK Ltd.
UKHW020056271124
451585UK00012B/1289